Adam's hands worked in concert with his mouth, molding Jackie's pliant softness against his hard muscles, traveling from her shoulders to her hips, kneeding and massaging her flesh into tingling awareness of the warm magic of his fingers and palms.

It seemed entirely natural when he lifted her into his arms to carry her to the couch in front of the fireplace, and when he laid her gently down, Jackie's arms pulled him with her until they were settled body against body among the soft cushions. In mutual agreement each undid the impeding buttons of the other's clothing until their upper bodies were bare to hungry eyes, hungry lips, and hungry hands. . . .

ABOUT THE AUTHOR

Jacqueline Ashley has lived in many places
during her marriage in connection to her
husband's job, including Hawaii, California,
New Jersey, and now currently in Kansas. She
began her writing career after recipients of her
personal correspondence begged her to write
a book. She's been happily writing romances
ever since!

Books by Jacqueline Ashley

HARLEQUIN AMERICAN ROMANCES

20-LOVE'S REVENGE
40-HUNTING SEASON

These books may be available at your local bookseller.

For a free catalog listing all titles currently available,
send your name and address to:

Harlequin Reader Service
P.O. Box 52040, Phoenix, AZ 85072-2040
Canadian address: Stratford, Ontario N5A 6W2

Hunting Season

JACQUELINE ASHLEY

Harlequin Books

TORONTO • NEW YORK • LONDON
AMSTERDAM • PARIS • SYDNEY • HAMBURG
STOCKHOLM • ATHENS • TOKYO • MILAN

Published January 1984

First printing November 1983

ISBN 0-373-16040-2

Printed in Canada

Chapter One

Jacqueline Afton Roth typed out an envelope to one of her publishers, inserted the article she'd just completed, and leaned wearily back in her chair, wishing her arms wouldn't feel like lumps of dead clay every time she completed one of her marathon writing spurts. She flexed her fingers to work out the kinks, then stretched her arms back over her head with tired satisfaction and yawned hugely to draw air into her cramped lungs.

Suddenly her eyes flew open in surprise, and a yelp of astonishment interrupted the yawn when her chair, instead of firmly supporting her back as usual, kept going back and back and back.

She just had time to throw her head to the side as she sensed the solid bulk of the table behind her rising to meet her skull, and when the crash of body and chair was over, she had a stomach full of armrest and a throbbing ache in her temple where it had collided with the unyielding hardwood floor.

"Damn!" she snarled with weak anger as she struggled to untangle herself from the sprawl of upholstery. Pain of any kind always made her angry, and if it was unexpected pain, it made her twice as angry. This time she had cause for the emotion on both counts, and, as usual, she expressed it verbally.

"Stupid chair! Why don't you pick on someone your own size!" she snarled at the offending chair after she'd gotten to her feet and stood eyeing it with malice while she rubbed her temple gently. A lump was starting to rise like an egg under the wisp of blond-streaked, ash-brown hair that shaded her profile.

Jackie reached down to right the chair and discovered it now had an odd tilt to the back that boded ill for future occupancy. Kneeling, she peered under its base to discover an empty hole where previously had resided a sturdy bolt designed, no doubt, to prevent just such an occurrence as had happened. Jackie shifted her eyes to the floor, searching for the missing bolt. There the little beggar was, resting complacently against the baseboard under the table, just as though it hadn't been an active participant in dumping her on her backside. She stretched out a hand to recover it, then turned it in her fingers and peered at it accusingly as though wanting it to tell her *why* it was there in her hand instead of in the chair, where it belonged.

Finally, she sighed and stood up again, tossing the bolt into an ashtray on her desk. She wasn't in the mood to try to fit it back into the chair at the moment, and she would probably need a screwdriver to tighten it securely, anyway, she thought with surly impatience as she turned on her heels to leave the room and cross the hall to the bathroom.

After opening the medicine cabinet, Jackie got out a bottle of witch hazel and a cotton ball and began to dab at her temple, wincing as the slight pressure brought forth a stabbing ache.

"I'll probably have a black eye tomorrow," she muttered under her breath as she replaced the witch hazel in the cabinet and tossed the cotton away.

When she returned her gaze to the mirror, Jackie searched her face anxiously. Sapphire-blue eyes set attractively under winged dark eyebrows stared back at her half-challengingly. Quelling the quiver in her firm stubborn little chin, Jackie scowled at her reflection. "So I had another accident," she addressed herself with a nonchalant defiance that didn't quite come off. "So what? That's all it was—an accident!"

The mocking curve of her sweet mobile mouth brought her attention to her lips. Matt had loved that mouth—had loved it and had known exactly how to make it curve up into laughter or pull down in anger. Dear, exasperating, totally satisfying Matt, who had married her and made her life whole for seven very short years, then disappeared into a black yawning grave, leaving her only half-alive.

"Stop it!" Jackie said the words more forcefully than she had meant to in her determination to short-circuit the trend of her thoughts. The echo of her ringing admonition to herself caused her to straighten her shoulders and firm her back resolutely. She turned away from her image in the mirror with a jerk and left the bathroom to cross to her bedroom, unfastening the buttons to her pale blue silk blouse as she went. After pulling it off abstractedly and tossing it onto the end of her bed, Jackie then unzipped her navy-blue slacks, stepped out of them, and tossed them to join the blouse. A glance at her bedside clock told her she would have to hurry to be on time for dinner with her friends.

Even as her body performed her will in selecting fresh clothing to put on, her mind flew rapidly over the events of the past two weeks, striving for an explanation as to why she should have started having accidents again after almost a year of peace. Jackie had descended into a deep depression after her husband, Matt, had been killed in an accident a year and a half ago, and she had thought it would never end. Gradually it had, turning instead into a numbed acceptance that permitted her to function while it provided no joy in living. And then a series of accidents had started. Neither she nor anyone else had thought much about them at first until, at a party she had been reluctantly dragooned into attending by some friends, Jackie had met Dr. Chelski.

Dr. Chelski was an elderly fatherly psychiatrist who had literally exuded security and warmth, wisdom and compassion. Jackie had somehow ended up in a corner with him, talking of this and that—nothing very consequential, as Jackie hadn't been in the mood to make much of a conversational effort. Someone— she couldn't even remember who it had been—had jokingly referred to her propensity for accidents, and Dr. Chelski had fixed his wise kindly eyes on her and begun a gentle probing.

That had been the beginning of several months of therapy, during the course of which Jackie had discovered that her so-called accidents were nothing more than her own attempt to join Matt in death.

"Well, I got over it, didn't I?" Jackie muttered to herself now as she slipped a soft jersey dress over her shoulders and pulled the back together to zip it. "So what if in the past two weeks I've nearly been electrocuted twice and then I tried to crush my skull today?"

There had been the radio on the shelf near the bathtub. She kept it there to soothe her nerves while she soaked out the stresses and strains of a day spent leeching her mind of appropriate phrases for each new article she wrote for the magazines. Two weeks earlier the nail holding the shelf had worked loose, and the radio had tumbled down to bounce off the edge of the bathtub before falling to the floor. Two inches—no more—had saved her from electrocution.

That doesn't prove a thing! Jackie thought rather desperately. *Didn't I move the shelf afterward to a less dangerous position? Doesn't that prove I don't want to die?*

"Yeah," she answered herself sarcastically. "Except that a week later you nearly electrocuted yourself with the toaster."

A piece of toast had broken off inside the grill, and Jackie had unthinkingly fished for it with a fork, forgetting to unplug the appliance beforehand. There had been a bright flash, but fortunately she had dropped the fork quickly enough to prevent being burned. "Wouldn't I have held on to the damn fork if I wanted to kill myself?" she asked her image now as she slipped on a pair of high-heeled sandals in front of her mirror, then left the bedroom to return to the bathroom to freshen her makeup and fix her hair.

Her scowl was mutinous as she pulled her hair back
from her forehead and fastened it into a French-style
bun at the center of the back of her head, then pulled
strands of the fine silky wisps over her temples and
ears. "I *know* I didn't remove that bolt from the
chair," she said with foreceful vehemence as she
tucked in the last pin. "That's not my style. Walking
off the edge of an unfilled swimming pool, yes. Anything requiring planning beforehand, no!"

Moments later, after grabbing her purse and jacket,
she marched resolutely out the door of her apartment,
having decided with grim determination to put her
uneasy thoughts behind her and enjoy the evening
with her friends if it took every ounce of willpower
she had.

The drive through the colorful precipitous streets
of San Francisco soothed her somewhat, and by the
time she walked into the unfashionable but homey
warmth of Luigi's, she was in a much better mood.
When she caught sight of the three women she was
joining seated at their favorite decrepit table, she
smiled and made her way toward them, thinking how
attractive, if radically different, her friends were.

Ceil, a cute, bouncy, deceptively petite, and even
more deceptively "dumb" blonde, was a successful
real estate broker with more sales to her credit than
many of her more sedate competitors. Beneath her
little-girl charm lay a thick layer of cynical realism.
She had seen too many unsavory aspects of human
nature in her sales work to be surprised by much,
and perhaps that was why she remained unmarried,
though she claimed it was because she had dis-

covered early on the advantages of playing the field as opposed to a steady diet of just one man.

Bess was Ceil's opposite in every way. She was the genuine homemaker type, complete with tall, successful, dominant husband and two children, one of each gender, just as she had always dreamed of, planned for, and thoroughly enjoyed. She was a naive dreamer, always creating lovely situations in her mind, thinking the best of everyone, her heart torn by all the cruel injustices in the world. Her long, silky brown hair curled charmingly around her heart-shaped face, framing soft brown eyes ready to swim with sympathetic tears at the slightest provocation.

Liv was a warm, maternal rock, calm, positive, and steady, with Ceil's realism tempered by compassion and Bess's optimism tempered by reality. She was a social worker, which required all of the clear-eyed, comforting humanity she possessed. She was single by choice, but there was a doctor "friend" in the background who provided all the male companionship she required. Liv made no effort to explain why their relationship had never led to marriage, and no one who knew her well ever made the mistake of asking her.

Jackie didn't know exactly where she fit into this disparate menagerie. She was a widow who had been more than happily married, and while she supposed someday a man *might* come along who could make her feel as wondrously satisfied as Matt had, she doubted it. A man who was capable of taking Matt's place would have to be very, very special, and they were not that thick on the ground. For that reason she had not dated since his death, never having been approached by anyone who could remotely compete with her deceased husband. She and Matt had been working, as well as emotional, partners, he a well-known newspaper reporter for a large San Francisco newspaper, she his silent helpmate.

Because of her outgoing personality and a certain sympathetic charm that made people trust and confide in her, Jackie had been of immense help to Matt in getting people to open up about themselves. When Matt was pressed for time to meet a deadline, she had sorted his notes and her own into workable order and prepared an outline from which he had written the story. In the process she had learned a great deal about the art of writing and had made contacts that were serving her well now. She never felt that Matt had deprived her of a career of her own because working with him had, in the beginning, shown her how much she needed to learn, and later, with his encouragement, she had used the lessons he taught her to hone her own skills. The two of them had made a formidable team and along the way had forged an integrated marriage that might not have been possible had they been pulling in opposite directions.

Matt's co-workers and editors had been well aware of the happy results of the partnership and after Matt's death, had pressed her to go to work for the newspaper full-time. Instead she had elected to freelance. The work was satisfying and interesting, gave her a steady income over and above what Matt had left her, made her feel useful, and kept her involved in the world around her. At the same time, because she was her own master, so to speak, she wasn't tied down to a rigid schedule and she felt she had the best of both worlds in such an arrangement. It couldn't compare with the one she had known with Matt, of course, but it was adequate.

Now, looking at the other three women at the table, Jackie supposed she was somewhat of a mixture of their types. She was not normally as cynical as Ceil, but she had seen enough of life that the emotion was not unknown to her. She could sympathize with Bess's causes without getting carried away to the point of tears, and, like Bess, she wanted children, though she didn't think she would ever *live* for them the way Bess seemed to. If asked to draw a comparison, she thought her character would be closest to Liv's, though without Liv's self-sacrificing nature, even though Liv made her sacrifices knowingly, rather than through being conned or used by others.

Jackie listened with barely suppressed amusement as Ceil held forth on local politics, heatedly defending the conservative candidate for mayor. "What do you mean, he's *cold*, Bess?" Ceil was saying indignantly. "Just because he wants to put some of our deadwood to work instead of letting them live off my taxes? That makes him *cold*?"

Bess's grave demeanor brought a slight smile to Jackie's lips. She knew what was coming. "Ceil, it's our duty to help those less fortunate than ourselves" was the predictable reply. "They're not all deadwood. Most of them are truly handicapped in some way. Can't you find it in your heart to pity them, instead of wanting to persecute them the way that man wants to do?"

Ceil threw up her hands and snorted in disgust. "Now he's a persecutor, no less! Did you hear that, Jackie? Liv? Can you picture that gorgeous hunk of man *persecuting* anyone, for heaven's sake?"

Liv put a comforting hand on Bess's arm and grinned at Ceil. "As a matter of fact, I can," she said with dry humor. "He looks very much the way I've always pictured the Marquis de Sade." And with a sly look at Jackie to clue her in, she added, "But that would appeal to you, wouldn't it, Ceil?" Her tone and question were greeted with laughter by the others, for they all knew Ceil's penchant for spectacularly flamboyant dark good looks.

Ceil smiled archly, not at all put out by the question. "What a good description," she said smugly, breaking into a chuckle at Bess's patently disapproving look. "I wonder how I could get a personal introduction to him?" she teased, hoping to provoke Bess further.

"Offer to work for his campaign, of course," Jackie put in, glad to get her mind off her own worrying thoughts. "Bat those eyelashes at him. You'll knock him off his feet in no time—literally!"

Her joke provoked more laughter, even from Ceil, who made no bones about the fact that she wore the thickest set of false eyelashes on the market, considering them a necessary business asset.

The talk drifted around and through a hundred different subjects after that, and it was only occasionally that Jackie's thoughts returned to what was uppermost in her mind—the recurring accidents. She caught Liv's discerning eyes on her from time to time and would make an effort to hide her preoccupation by joining in the talk more assertively.

It was as they were leaving the restaurant that Liv took the opportunity to draw her aside. "Jackie, you look a bit tired and worried. Are you working too hard?"

Jackie smiled ruefully and shrugged. It was a handy excuse, and she took what was offered gratefully. "Maybe so," she agreed lightly. "The assignments *are* coming in rather more steadily than usual."

Liv looked satisfied and offered some standard advice. "Why don't you take a vacation? You haven't been anywhere since—" She broke off, biting her lip with regret that she had inadvertently brought up Matt's death, then hurried on. "You should get away for a while, honey. A change of scene would do you worlds of good."

Jackie found the idea only slightly appealing. She and Matt had loved to travel, but how much fun would it be to go anywhere alone? she wondered. Nevertheless, she replied with a good simulation of enthusiasm. "Great idea! I'll give it some thought."

"Don't think—do!" Liv smiled warmly at her as she uttered the half-scolding words. "You need a break."

Bess and Ceil joined them then, and the four of them left the restaurant to walk down the street to the corner light. Luigi's didn't have valet parking, so they all parked in a commercial lot across the street. Their chatter ran nonstop as they joined a small group waiting for the light to change to green. Jackie was standing right on the edge of the curb when the crowd surged suddenly to make room for a roller-skating teenager skimming down the street at top speed. Before Jackie knew what was happening she found herself pitched forward into the street and straight into the path of an oncoming pickup truck.

Suddenly there was the screech of brakes, the screams of her friends and the other onlookers, and the sickening fear of death that rose to her throat to choke off her breath as she glimpsed the huge cab of the truck bearing down on her. Jackie closed her eyes hard to shut out the vision, knowing there wasn't time to rise from her hands and knees and get out of the way. And then it was over.

She felt hands grasping her to help her up and opened her eyes to see the front bumper of the truck mere inches away from where she knelt. Feeling dazed and almost disbelieving that she had escaped what she had thought was certain death, she allowed the helping hands to lift her and then was confronted by the hysterical ranting of the elderly man who had jumped from his truck to accost her.

"Lady, why you jump in front of me like that?" he screamed at her. "You no want to *live* anymore?"

His angry question focused her attention, and Jackie brought her head up sharply to stare at him. "Yes!" she yelled back at him fiercely, the blood finally pumping in her veins again and her adrenaline soaring. "Yes, I want to live!" she repeated forcefully, realizing she meant it wholeheartedly.

As she said the words she determined that she was

going to find out if her subconscious meant them as well. It was time to visit Dr. Chelski and discover if her mind was playing tricks on her again, the way it had after Matt's death.

"You are too thin, too tired, and too nervous," Dr. Chelski said in his deep, gentle, fatherly voice, which now held a hint of admonition. "Why is that?"

Jackie took a deep breath before replying, remembering affectionately that Dr. Chelski always did like to get right to the point and considered conventional greetings a waste of time. "It's no fun eating alone, my work load has surged recently, and—I seem to have been having a few accidents lately." Jackie mumbled the last part, quickly averting her eyes from the sharpened look in the elderly psychiatrist's discerning brown eyes and the frown that tugged at his full lips beneath his white beard.

"Now, why is that, I wonder?" he said musingly, half-inviting, half-commanding her to join him in speculation.

Jackie shrugged. "I haven't a clue," she admitted. "I could swear that this time they really *are* just accidents. They don't feel the same as last time—I mean *I* don't feel the same when they happen."

"Oh?" He seemed encouraged by her words. "And how do you feel when they happen?"

"Scared silly," Jackie replied promptly with a shudder of remembrance at her close call with the truck the night before, when she had been pushed into the street by the movement of the crowd waiting for the light to change.

"Ah...now, that is encouraging." Dr. Chelski positively beamed at her. "Still...." He got up from his chair behind the large mahogany desk and walked around it, motioning Jackie to move to the comfortable reclining chair in one corner of his office. "Why don't we check out your subconscious and see how she is doing? We both know how resourceful and naughty she has been in the past, and she may be getting restless again, hmmm?"

Jackie eyed the recliner with resignation, having suspected before she walked in here that Dr. Chelski would want to resort to hypnosis, but still unable to quell the slight sense of apprehension she always felt at being placed in someone's power this way, even her beloved Dr. Chelski's. Indeed, if it had been anyone but him, she didn't think she could ever have developed the requisite trust to have submitted to the process, though she knew it was a valuable tool and had helped pinpoint her problem in the past.

Still, a bare few minutes later, it seemed, Dr. Chelski was bringing her out of it, and she felt so relaxed and comfortable, it was an effort to glance down at her watch and see that actually a half hour had passed.

"Well?" she asked sleepily, eyeing Dr. Chelski's calm satisfied face warily to see if she could detect his reaction to her revelations under hypnosis. "How is she?" She was referring to her subconscious, of course, whom she and Dr. Chelski invariably referred to as though discussing an entirely separate person, a practice that had helped Jackie cope in the past but which now seemed rather eerily inappropriate.

"I think she has decided to let you remain in control," Dr. Chelski answered with satisfaction. "She doesn't want to die anymore, either."

"Thank God!" Jackie said with feeling, and then a second later, "But what about the accidents?"

Dr. Chelski shrugged, bunching his huge shoulders in a comical gesture. "So Freud was wrong, maybe?" he suggested with a grin. "And maybe there is such a thing as real accidents?"

"Geez, I don't know whether to be grateful or sorry," Jackie said quite truthfully. "I mean, I'm glad I don't want to die anymore, but getting knocked off by a real accident isn't any more appealing than planning it subconsciously when you get right down to it!"

"True," Dr. Chelski agreed. "But I think we can cut down on the possibility of that happening, as well."

"How?" Jackie sounded gloomy. However discouraging the thought that she might have been wanting to join her deceased husband Matt again had been, it was at least an explanation and could be dealt with, with Dr. Chelski's help. But real accidents were just that—accidents. And how did one develop a plan to avoid them? she wondered.

"You need a change of scene, Jackie," Dr. Chelski said. "You have, by your own admission, been working too hard and not eating properly. It's time you dropped out for a while."

"Dropped out?" Jackie was puzzled.

He nodded his leonine head. "Took a vacation, scrammed, got a new perspective. In short—dropped out."

Jackie stared at him for a moment, then sighed. "You too, huh?"

"Pardon?" It was his turn to look puzzled.

"A friend of mine told me the same thing last night."

"Then he must be a good friend," Dr. Chelski said with satisfaction.

"It's a she," Jackie replied even more gloomily.

"Ah...and that's another thing," Dr. Chelski asserted. "Have you started dating yet?"

"No!" Short and sulky.

"Why not?" Stern and accusatory.

"Don't start with me!" Jackie said with irritated warning. "Just call me picky and let it go at that."

"Jackie...Jackie..." Dr. Chelski gave a huge sigh of forbearance. "Why can't you accept that there are other men in this world who can make you just as happy as Matt did?"

"Ha!" Jackie said half under her breath.

"Ha, indeed," Dr. Chelski replied with wry sternness. "As long as you have your present attitude, I admit the possibility of your finding someone is remote. It's very hard for a living man to compete with a ghost. Especially when the ghost's keeper won't let him rest in peace."

Jackie glared at him. He glared back. "Let Matt *go*, Jackie," he ordered in a no-nonsense tone. "Get on with your own life. Get married again. Have some kids. Write that novel you're always talking about and never start!"

Jackie seized the mention of the novel as a diversion. She didn't want to sit and listen for an additional half hour while Dr. Chelski admonished her to go out and find another Matt when he had no conception of how difficult that would be. "I suppose I could combine a vacation with a start on the novel," she offered with purposeful abstraction, as though she were thinking out loud. She was delighted when her diversion worked.

"Excellent idea!" Dr. Chelski beamed, then he frowned. "As long as you don't turn it into a marathon working holiday that will leave you even more tired than you are now."

"Oh, no...no..." Jackie said innocently. "I wouldn't do that." She furrowed her brow in thought again, getting caught up more seriously in the idea of a working vacation. It *would* be nice to get out of the rat race for a while and have a complete change of scene, she reasoned. The trick would be to find the right place.

"Pace yourself," Dr. Chelski advised. "Set up a routine, but keep it loose and easy. You have a tendency toward overwork, you realize. You must work more on relaxing." He looked startled for a moment at his inadvertent choice of words, then grinned charmingly. "Think of it as a project you have to accomplish—learning to relax, that is—then it will seem more acceptable to you."

"I am *not* a workaholic!" Jackie flared at him.

Two huge bushy eyebrows rose at her skeptically. "No?" he asked with suspicious innocence.

"No! At least I never was until—until—" Jackie's protests got weaker.

"Until Matt died, and that's all there was in your life that had any meaning," Dr. Chelski supplied with soft compassion.

Jackie sulked, then slowly relented. "Maybe," she mumbled, her tone still denoting that she was not fully convinced, though, in truth, she was. Then she eyed Dr. Chelski's kindly expression with humor. "I must be well now," she said dryly, "because you don't even try to hide your sneaky psychology with tact anymore."

He beamed at her again. "You were never unwell, Jackie," he scoffed. "You just didn't know how to handle grief. A lot of people don't."

"I'll bet a lot of people don't try to join their departed loved ones in the grave, either," Jackie replied with rueful acceptance.

"You'd be surprised," Dr. Chelski grunted. "And you weren't trying hard enough to have a real death wish. You were flirting but uncommitted." With a purposeful glint in his eyes he continued. "That reminds me of your little diversion tactic a few minutes ago. Right now I'd be happy if you would even consent to *flirt* where men are concerned. Commitment will come in its own due time, but not unless you start the process."

Jackie sighed wearily and covered her eyes with her hand. "Oh, geez, will you get off that?" she asked with a hint of pleading. "It's not that simple."

"No," Dr. Chelski agreed. "Love is never that simple. It is only necessary."

Jackie removed her hand from her eyes and looked at him skeptically. "Come, now, Dr. Chelski," she scoffed. "There are tons of people who remain unmarried and live perfectly happy lives."

Dr. Chelski looked straight into her eyes and said

very softly, "But not you, my dear. Never you. You are a giver and you need a receptacle to give *to*. You have such a wealth of love inside you that to me, it would be a sin to deprive some fortunate man of the happiness you know so well how to provide. Your Matt was a very, very lucky man." Then, abruptly changing moods from his sincere observations to sly innocence, he added almost abstractedly with a heavy sigh, "But if you want to be selfish enough to deny someone else a happy marriage..." He shrugged fatalistically.

Torn between a choked-up gratitude over his obviously sincere admiration for her ability to make a prospective husband happy and an outraged sense of being manipulated, Jackie opened her mouth to say something, closed it again, and ended up half-glaring, half-grinning at the sweet old man facing her who was as diabolical as Machiavelli. "Thanks!" she finally got out.

"You're welcome," he said with a benevolent look that made her want to laugh and cry at the same time.

"What do you want?" she asked resignedly.

"A promise," he answered promptly.

"What sort of promise?" she asked suspiciously.

"First, that you'll take the vacation—"

"What do you mean, first?" Jackie interjected with a snap. "You said *a* promise."

He waved that aside. "Semantics, semantics," he said airily. "Second, that if a man even one-*third* as acceptable to you as Matt makes a pass, you won't cut him off. You have to start *somewhere*."

"Sez who?" Jackie muttered mutinously.

"Sez me," he responded firmly, his lip curling with distaste at uttering such mongrel English. As a foreign-born citizen who had worked very hard to perfect his English, he found it very hard to accept some native Americans' tendency to bastardize it.

Jackie thought furiously for a moment, not wanting to disappoint him, but totally unable to contemplate playing the games most single men and women engaged in as a matter of course, but which seemed utterly inadequate when compared to the relationship she had had with Matt. Then her brow cleared as out of the blue she came up with a solution to the problem, as well as to the problem of where she would go for her vacation.

Smiling sweetly, she said with demure acceptance, "Very well...I agree."

Dr. Chelski looked taken aback for a moment at his easy victory, but Jackie looked so innocent, he squelched his unworthy suspicions. He knew she was honest to the core and he decided to take her word as befitted a gentleman. "Good! Good!" he chortled gleefully, causing Jackie to have a twinge of conscience at deceiving him, but only a twinge.

Glancing hastily at her watch—Jackie wanted to get out of there before her anything but mentally dull mentor decided to delve into details about her forthcoming vacation—she began to gather up her purse and her jacket, smiling happily at Dr. Chelski all the while.

"I'm so glad I came to see you again," she chattered gaily. "It's such relief to know that instead of being on the verge of doing away with myself, I'm merely tired and therefore careless, or just in the wrong place at the wrong time. Thank you, Dr. Chelski. I don't know what I'd have done without you in the last year and a half."

Dr. Chelski lumbered to his feet, his face creased in a smile. "It has been a pleasure to help you, my dear. I confess you are one of my favorite patients. So intelligent, so basically healthy emotionally, so willing to take my advice."

Jackie caught the wince struggling to take possession of her face and turned it into an even wider smile. "I'll take all the compliments I can get," she tossed off airily. "In fact, I'll promise to come in weekly again if you'll promise to spend our hour whispering sweet nothings in my ear."

Chuckling, Dr. Chelski wrapped one of his huge arms around her shoulders and gave her a hug. "No need for that," he protested heartily, "though I do want to hear from you when you get back from your vacation—out of curiosity, you understand. As a friend, not professionally." His eyes glowed with kind appreciation of her attributes as a woman as he escorted her to the door. "But as for sweet nothings, I'm hoping that by the time you come back you'll have a younger, sexier man to provide those for you. You deserve a bushel of them."

"Thank you, kind sir," Jackie murmured demurely, dropping her eyes as much to hide her doubt that such an event would come to pass as to give the appearance of being embarrassed.

"Good-bye, Dr. Chelski." She took her leave with sadness, yet relief, that she was not likely to be seeing him again.

"Good-bye Jackie," he echoed. "Good hunting."

Jackie smiled mischievously, but once the door to Dr. Chelski's office had closed behind her, her smile turned into a grimace as she reflected that while Dr. Chelski might be the wisest, kindest man she knew, he was *such* an innocent where love was concerned. Good hunting, indeed!

Chapter Two

It was a long drive from San Francisco to Pinedale, Wyoming, but the gorgeous scenery and perfect September weather helped the long hours behind the wheel pass pleasantly. Jackie spent the last night of the trip in Idaho Falls, Idaho, planning to get an early start the following morning, make a short detour through Jackson, Wyoming, and reach Pinedale in the afternoon.

As she climbed out of the car in the parking space at the motel she'd chosen, the pure balmy air wrapped her like a benevolent cloak, and she took a deep breath of utter release. The sheer uneventfulness of the trip so far, plus the lovely weather, added a dash of impetus to her inherent feeling that Liv and Dr. Chelski had been right about her needing to drop out for a while. Not that Dr. Chelski would approve of *where* she planned to drop, since there were unlikely to be any men around a lonely mountain cabin. But if any likely males should turn up, and if they were even one-third as attractive to her as Matt had been, she would live up to her promise to Dr. Chelski to the

letter, Jackie thought with sly self-righteousness, secure in the knowledge that such an eventuality was so
remote as to be nonexistent.

She had wasted no time starting the wheels rolling
to make the trip possible after her session with Dr.
Chelski had convinced her that the idea had merit.
Her inquiry about the cabin where she had spent several days with her parents during her teens had resulted in a favorable reply, and she considered that a
good omen, since the hunting season was due to begin soon in Wyoming, and normally the cabin would
have been booked months in advance. Fortunately,
the owner had just received a cancellation, and since
she wanted the cabin for a minimum of three months,
he had been delighted to rent it to her.

Jackie didn't quite know why the idea of spending
time there appealed to her so strongly. Perhaps it was
because it had associations with her happy, uncompli-
cated childhood, before love and grief had lifted her
to the heights and thrown her into the depths of despair so precipitously. Nor did she know why the
remembrance of it had popped into her mind so fortu-
itously in Dr. Chelski's office when she had been
searching for a way to *appear* to agree with his asser-
tion that she needed to find another man to take
Matt's place. Nevertheless, she was exceedingly grateful that she had remembered the place and that it
filled her requirements admirably.

She had been in her teens when she had accompanied her parents on a trip to Yellowstone Park. On the
way they had discovered the cabin and spent several
peaceful days there just enjoying the quiet and the

magnificent scenery. The landscapes in the northwestern corner of Wyoming had suited her photographer father right down to the ground, Jackie remembered with fond affection. His hunting had all been done with a camera, not with the rifle so many visitors here relied upon for entertainment, she thought with a downward curl of her lip in disgust.

The cabin was nestled in the Bridger-Teton National Forest south of Jackson and several miles from Pinedale, amid splendid surroundings that had tugged at her senses all the time she and her parents had spent there. It was somewhat primitive as she recalled, with only one bedroom, a bath, and a combination living room and kitchen. She had had to sleep on a couch in front of the wood-burning fireplace, as her parents took the bedroom, but she hadn't minded. The flames had provided her endless entertainment and comfort as she lay each night waiting for sleep, toasty warm and content with her environment.

Jackie hoped they would provide her with inspiration for the book she planned to write while she was here. The isolated surroundings would provide her with the privacy and peace she required in order to relax.

After a refreshing shower and a leisurely dinner, Jackie stretched out between clean sheets and picked up a novel she had brought along, but the relaxation she sought was already making itself felt, and before she knew it, she was opening her eyes to another glorious morning. With a smile of anticipation she was out of bed and dressed before getting on her way again.

The miles sped by, and the scenery was so lovely, she felt like stopping every few moments to snap pictures, but she disciplined her impulses sternly, or else she'd never reach the cabin before nightfall. Golden rolling wheat fields dotted the landscape on the Idaho/Wyoming border, filling the horizon with glorious patterns. She couldn't resist stopping at least once when she saw a scenic turnout that provided a spectacular view of the Snake River far below, winding its way through small islands in serene majesty. Then she was into the mountains and catching her breath unconsciously at the steep grades as she climbed, then descended into the valley that held the charming town of Jackson, Wyoming.

Jackie drove a short distance past Jackson on the way to Yellowstone, reliving memories of the trip she'd taken with her parents, then turned back, pulling to the side of the road occasionally to gaze at the majestic Tetons. When her stomach told her it was lunchtime, she spent a delightful half hour walking the wooden sidewalks of Jackson before settling on a restaurant for a meal. After lunch, she couldn't resist buying herself a pair of western boots, elaborately stenciled with bucking broncos, a warm sheepskin jacket, gloves, and a western hat. She returned to her car, sporting a wide grin at her own foolishness, but she refused to spend much time deriding herself for succumbing to the western atmosphere. She felt much too good to spoil her mood.

As she got on her way again she rolled down the window to let the sun-warmed air caress her hair and cheeks with all its pure sensuality. The road curved up into the mountains again with more spectacular scenery, and before she knew it, she had reached Pinedale.

Jackie was pleasantly tired by the time she had fetched the key to the cabin, visited the grocer to lay in enough supplies to last her a week or so, and located the winding country road that would take her to the cabin. She drove as fast as she dared, wanting to get all her things carried in and put away before darkness descended, so she could eat her first meal snug and cozy before a fire in the fireplace, secure in her isolation and letting the rest of the world go on its merry way without her.

Finally, after a precarious journey on a pot-holed, very narrow lane that struck off from the scarcely better country road, she spotted the cabin nestling in a stand of trees and drew up to it with a sigh of relief. It looked just the same as she remembered it, and she could feel her heart expanding with anticipation of spending the next several weeks there.

The cabin had electricity, she was relieved to find, as it hadn't when she had visited it before with her parents. There was a small shed off to the side that emitted a humming noise, so she supposed there was a generator in there to provide lights and electricity for the refrigerator and heating, since there were no poles to be seen anywhere, just a line from the shed to the cabin.

Inside there were a few small changes: a new couch to replace the one she remembered, a new kitchen table and chairs in a pleasing wooden rustic style, and a new refrigerator and a stove. The rest of the furniture was the same, carved out of logs and upholstered in country patterns that added cheer to the atmosphere. The bathroom had an old claw-footed bath and an elderly sink that were functional, if not in the latest style.

All in all Jackie was more than pleased with what she found, since she had expected to have to live much more primitively than it was apparent would be necessary. She carried in groceries and stocked the refrigerator and cupboards, brought in fresh linens and towels she had brought to make the bed and stock the bathroom, and by early evening she was settled in and happily cooking toast, scrambled eggs, and bacon and had brewed fresh coffee, promising herself a more elaborate meal the next day, when she wouldn't be so tired.

As she sat before the gently crackling fire and sipped her coffee after cleaning the kitchen, Jackie reflected contentedly that she had been right to go there. She hadn't felt so relaxed and comfortable for so long, she had almost forgotten what getting away from the rat race could do for one. Yawning hugely, she stood up to rinse her cup and indulge in a long soak in the claw-footed bathtub before donning a long flannel gown that covered her from head to toe and was deliciously warm and soft. She stuck her feet in old, decrepit furry houseshoes and sat down at the antique dresser to braid her long hair for the night. She was making the last loop at the end of her braid when she heard the alarming sound of a backfiring truck driving up the lane to the cabin.

Jackie froze. What on earth! No one should have been coming up here at this time of night. The lane petered out barely a mile past the cabin—the owner had told her that. The owner! Could it be him? Had he forgotten something? But what? Surely they had discussed everything she needed to know this afternoon she thought.

For the first time her sense of isolation ceased to be comforting. What if it wasn't the owner? What if it was a nefarious character used to visiting the cabin for some unscrupulous purpose?

As she heard the vehicle stop outside her eyes shifted hurriedly to one of her suitcases lying open on a small holder at the end of the bed. It contained a pistol of Matt's she had brought along on impulse, not really dreaming she could ever have a use for it. She didn't even know how to load it but had simply dropped a clip of shells into the case, intending to figure it out somehow if she ever felt the need for protection. Perhaps just the *sight* of it would be enough to discourage any trespassers, she thought with panicky indecision as she heard a step on the porch.

The front doorknob rattled, and she heard a soft curse from whoever had approached the door. After grabbing her robe, she slipped it on haphazardly and belted it with trembling fingers. A dash to the suitcase produced the pistol, which she lifted gingerly and dropped into the capacious pocket of the robe. Then she slipped silently out of the bedroom and approached the door with quite a bit of trepidation as to what she should do when she got there. The only thing she was sure of was that she was not about to open it.

The knob rattling had ceased, and she heard steps

crossing the front porch and descending the three steps to the ground. She was about to expend a sigh of relief—perhaps whoever it was had given up and was leaving—when she remembered that she had left the bedroom light on, and if whoever it was circled the cabin, he would be sure to see it through the curtain and deduce that there was an occupant. But maybe that was a good thing, she thought indecisively. He might leave then.

Jackie listened hopefully for the sound of the truck engine starting up, but the only things that greeted her ears were the sounds of the night and, eventually, the sound of steps returning to the front of the cabin. Whoever it was made no effort to be stealthy, but clomped up the steps again and approached the door with steady purpose. Jackie didn't know whether to feel good or bad about the intruder's lack of caution.

Suddenly there was the sound of a tremendous thudding knock on the door. Jackie jumped a foot in reaction to it, but before she was over that upset the sound of a deep masculine voice brought her heart into her mouth.

"Open up in there! Whoever you are, you're not supposed to be there, and if you don't open this door immediately, I'm going to get the sheriff!"

Jackie gulped in astonishment, unable to fathom whether this was some ploy in order to get her to open the door so whoever it was could rob her—or worse—or whether the person was legitimately outraged that she should be staying in the cabin. She approached a step closer to the door, wringing her hands in agitation, not knowing what to do. The voice was not that of the owner, she was certain of that. In any case, the owner *knew* she had a right to be there.

"You've got one minute left before I go for the sheriff!" The threatening, overwhelmingly masculine quality of the voice was intimidating, but there was also a cultured, educated tone that was incongruent with Jackie's picture of a lout who meant her physical harm. It was that tone that decided her. She moved closer and opened her mouth to speak, but the other voice spoke first.

"All right, on your own head be it, then! We'll see how you like being brought up on trespassing charges—or maybe even robbery! I'll be back with the sheriff pretty damn quick, and if you know what's good for you, you'll clear out by then!"

There was the sound of retreating steps, and for a moment Jackie was tempted to let the man carry out his threat. If he was legitimate, wouldn't he look pretty silly dragging the sheriff out on a wild-goose chase, though? She smiled nervously and cleared her throat "Wait a minute!" she called hoarsely. She heard the steps pause briefly, then return.

"Who the hell is in there?" The voice showed astonishment. "A woman alone? Or is your man too cowardly to come out himself?"

Jackie debated about letting the man think she really did have a husband stashed protectively away in the cabin, but then she changed her mind. Aggressiveness seemed like the best bet under the circumstances.

"For your information, Mr.—whoever you are—I have rented this cabin. *I* am not trespassing, *you* are!

Now please go away and leave me alone to enjoy it!''

There! That sounded pretty cool and confident, she congratulated herself. But not for long.

"A likely story!" the voice sneered back at her. "Why would any woman want to rent this cabin clear out in the boonies and stay in it alone? You'd better get your husband and clear out of there before I lose my temper!"

Jackie was losing her fear in the heat of her growing irritation. The man sounded as though he were used to issuing orders and having them obeyed by a passel of slaves. Who did he think he was, anyway? she asked.

"It's none of your business *why* I rented this cabin," she shouted back at him with cold hostility. "The fact of the matter is, I *have* rented it, and *you* are trespassing. You can go get the sheriff and anyone else you like if you don't believe me. Better yet, go get John Reardon, the owner. He's the one I paid my money to and he's the one who will send you packing. Now, will you please leave and let me get some sleep?"

There was silence for a few seconds, and Jackie began to wonder if the man was going to take her suggestion. It would mean a lot of trouble for everyone, she fumed, but at least it might be worth it to see the arrogant clown get his comeuppance.

"*When* did you pay John Reardon for this cabin?" The sneer was gone, but the skeptical tone was still apparent.

"Two weeks ago. I wired him the money," Jackie said with a hint of triumphant condescension in her voice. "He had a cancellation," she added somewhat unnecessarily, perhaps trying to add more veracity to her statement by adding detail, though why she was standing in her bathrobe trying to convince some unknown belligerent that she had a right to be where she was, was beyond her. She should have just let him go for the sheriff.

"Well, that's interesting," the voice replied, this time with irritated exasperation, "because I paid *my* money for this cabin, too, and I *didn't* cancel!"

He sounded so self-righteously indignant that Jackie found herself believing him despite all her best instincts. For a moment she even felt sorry for him if what he said was true, but that didn't mean she was prepared to pack up and move out to accommodate him. Nor was she prepared to believe him to the extent that she was going to let him in.

Unconsciously she had moved closer to the door, and then she leaned her shoulder against it and crossed one leg over the other. A sudden vision of the ludicrous picture the two of them probably presented crossed her mind, and she smiled involuntarily, but her voice was crisply discouraging when she spoke again.

"I'm afraid you'll have to take that up with John Reardon," she said in a no-nonsense voice. "If there's been some mix-up, that's too bad, but possession is still nine tenths of the law, and since I'm in possession, I'm afraid you'll have to find some other accommodation for the night."

"Oh, hell..." There was no mistaking the frustrated anger the stranger was feeling. "Lady, I've been driving since six o'clock this morning to get here, and it's at least eighty miles to a decent motel. I'm not about to get back into that bone-crusher and start out again—not when I've already paid for a bed right here!"

Jackie straightened up and glared at the door. "Well, you'll have to, won't you?" she said coldly. "If you think I'm going to let a strange man in here at this time of night, you're crazy!" She relented in her tone then somewhat, but only infinitesimally. "Besides, there's only one bed, so it wouldn't do any good if I did let you in."

There was the briefest of pauses before the stranger came back at her, his tone changing to one of controlled reasonableness. "But there's a floor isn't there?" he said almost coaxingly, as though he were speaking to a child to whom he was suggesting a treat if the child would only cooperate. "I could sleep there, and in the morning we could get this straightened out."

Jackie cursed her stupidity in even mentioning the *idea* of letting him in. "No, you couldn't, and there's nothing *to* straighten out," she said with gritting patience. "I've paid my money and I'm staying, and I'm not letting some stranger out of the night in here to rob me, or—or—whatever!" She cursed herself again for perhaps putting ideas into his head and was paradoxically incensed when she heard his soft, rather nasty chuckle.

"Lady, believe me, you have no worries on that score. As tired as I am now, *you'd* have to do the whatever, if there was any of it done. I'm as respectable a man as you're ever likely to meet, and I assure you robbing you, raping you, or even talking to you is the last thing on my mind at the moment.''

Unconvinced, Jackie fired back at him. "If you're so tired, then what was all that talk about going for the sheriff? If you were willing to do that, why can't you make the trip to find a motel room instead?" Let him put *that* in his pipe and smoke it, she thought smugly, and then couldn't believe that she was standing there holding a conversation with a total stranger in the middle of the night, clad in nightgown and bathrobe, and actually *enjoying* trying to get his goat. She must be out of her mind! she thought.

Jackie heard a long-suffering sigh and then again the controlled patience. "I wasn't actually going for the sheriff. I was going to drive off and park for a while until whoever was in here cleared out. I figured you were some hunter taking advantage of free accommodations, since this place is so isolated." And then he added more forcefully, "Lady, haven't you got an iota of compassion? It's cold as hell out here. I'm about to drop where I stand from fatigue. I swear to you I won't harm you if you'll just let me in so I can get some sleep!"

There was a despairing note in his voice that softened Jackie's irritation with him, but was not enough to make her lose all common sense.

"I'm sorry," she said almost kindly, "but I really can't take your word for your good intentions, can I?" She spoke reasonably, willing him to understand her predicament, then thought again that she was insane to care. What did he expect, anyway? If she were his wife, she would have bet a dollar to a hole in a dough-nut that he would have had a very different attitude about the advisability of a lone woman letting a completely strange man into her cabin to share accommodations. "You'll just have to find yourself somewhere else to stay," she said more firmly. "Can't you sleep in your truck?"

"Sure!" he said with exaggerated sarcasm. "It's only going to get down to about thirty degrees tonight. If I'm lucky, I'll only lose a couple of toes instead of dying of exposure!"

That was too much, Jackie thought with a hardening of her heart. If he thought he could play on her sympathies, it was just too bad. She ignored the small twinge of guilt his words had managed to inspire and decided to finish the ridiculous conversation. "Too bad," she said hardheartedly. "I guess you'll just have to find a hotel, then, won't you? As for me, I'm going to bed. *Good* night!"

There was silence from the other side of the door, and after a moment Jackie heard the thumping on the wooden porch that indicated the man was going away. She didn't move until she heard the engine of the truck start up, then she heaved a sigh of relief and returned to the bedroom to get ready for bed.

She couldn't help grinning to herself when she reviewed the preceding conversation in her mind. Who would have thought such a thing could happen here in the wilds of Wyoming in such total isolation? She thought she had left civilization behind, only to be besieged by one of its ill-tempered denizens right in the middle of nowhere.

Jackie climbed in between the clean sheets and pulled up the warm quilt around her shoulders, feeling safe and snug and just a teensy bit sorry for the man she had sent off into the night. She hoped he wouldn't have to drive *too* far before finding a motel, even if his manners did leave a lot to be desired and he probably didn't deserve her commiseration.

Oh, well, she thought sleepily as she reached up to switch off the bedside lamp, maybe she could use the incident in one of her stories someday. Not that anyone would believe it! A small chuckle escaped her lips as she snuggled down in the comfortable bed and pictured her irate visitor driving cursing through the night, looking for somewhere to stay, and all because some fool woman wouldn't invite him in, as though he were Prince Charming, to share her bed.

Chapter Three

Muffled thunder woke Jackie from a sound refreshing sleep, and she opened her eyes to a gray morning and the sight of rain streaming gently down the panes of the bedroom window. Far from depressing her, however, the weather brought a sleepy smile of smug satisfaction to her softened lips. She snuggled farther under the covers, enjoying the thought of drifting back to sleep to the accompaniment of the sound of rain for as long as she liked. There were no deadlines to meet, no telephones to answer, there was no *reason* to deny herself the luxury of sheer laziness, at least not for this one day.

She was still half-asleep, thoughts drifting in and out of her mind—thoughts that were almost dreams. She remembered how she and Matt had loved to lie abed on mornings like this when they fell on a weekend. They would make love leisurely, enjoying the warmth of each other's body, the satisfaction of knowing they were completely in tune physically and spiritually. Then they would talk without urgency of things that were on their minds, making plans, discussing anything and everything, enjoying the intimacy and relaxation that came so effortlessly when they were together.

For almost the first time the remembrances were easy ones—warm and tender and without the sharp pain of loss that had been her companion for so many months. The loss was there, of course. How could it be otherwise when her body felt longings that could no longer be assuaged by the one man who knew every response she was capable of and who was so expert at evoking them? How could it be otherwise when there was no one to tell her thoughts, no one to listen to, no one to share a loving glance of amusement or perception, agreement or disagreement? she wondered. And there had been disagreements. She and Matt had been compatible, but each was strongly individualistic. It had been inevitable that there would be clashes, but the clashes had been minor, almost enjoyable. She had even suspected that Matt had deliberately provoked them at times, enjoying her spirited reactions and enjoying even more the loving that had followed when they would make up.

Jackie sighed in her half-conscious state of remembrance, knowing somehow that though she would never forget Matt or what they had had together, she was on the verge of a final healing. The memories were more sweet than hurtful at last. She was going to be all right...really all right. She was certain of it.

She was drifting back into total unconsciousness when she became aware of a sound that seemed, if not out of place, at least more insistent than it had any right to be. Irritated, she swam up out of the darkness to place it. Running water. That was it, she thought with groggy perception. She opened her eyes to look at the rain on the window. It was a gentle rain, certainly not heavy enough to make such a noise. Was there a leak in the roof, perhaps? An overflowing gutter? she thought.

The second awakening was total, and Jackie scowled when she realized she was to be denied the pleasure of a morning in bed. But there was no use lying there just for the sake of it when she knew she wouldn't be able to go back to sleep, and if there *was* a leak somewhere, she had better check it and get John Reardon to fix it before the winter descended in full force, she knew.

After throwing back the covers, shivering at the onslaught of cold air that hit her body, Jackie rose to find her robe and slippers. She would visit the bathroom first, put on some coffee, and then look for that damn leak. She could still hear the steady running of water, and the force of it puzzled her. It sounded more like a wide-open faucet than a leak, and it seemed to be coming from the bathroom, too. How appropriate, she thought with wry resentment, still disgruntled at having her rest broken.

Shuffling her feet in her slippers, her eyes half-closed and bleary with sleep, Jackie left the bedroom and approached the closed door to the bathroom. The sound was definitely stronger now, and she could only hope that if there *was* a leak, it would be over the bathtub or the sink so that any damage it was causing would be minimal. Jackie opened the door, a worried frown creasing her forehead, her mouth pulled down in the resentful expression of a night person being forced to face a new day far too early to be comfortable.

The sight that met her eyes—indeed, the *eyes* that met her own startled ones in the mirror over the sink directly across from the door—brought a shriek to her lips. The man who stood with his naked back to her, his face half-covered in shaving lather, winced at the sound. He uttered a short expletive and started to turn toward her, but Jackie was already backing away on legs galvanized by fear. She didn't care that the man didn't look like her preconceived notion of a burglar or a rapist. She only noted that his obvious stature— he had to be well over six feet and with the muscle to go with the frame—precluded any brave thoughts she had ever had of facing down an opponent in a situation of this kind. The only thing that might stop someone with his bulk was a bullet, and she wasn't even certain a bullet would be effective enough to save her.

Spinning on her heels was a mistake. The furry slippers weren't made for spinning. They stayed where they were while Jackie stumbled out of them, and, her feet flying over the cold wooden floor, she ran for the bedroom, slamming the door behind her and racing for the suitcase that contained Matt's gun. It wasn't there! She wasted seconds in her panic-stricken state looking for it before she remembered it was still in her bathrobe pocket, weighing the material down with its reassuring bulk. She reached in a hand to get it, but it caught on the overlapping flap of the pocket and wouldn't come out.

Meanwhile, she heard the creak of the door opening behind her and was almost frantic in her effort to get the gun out of the pocket. Finally, it was free—she had torn the pocket—and she spun around to hold it in both shaking hands, pointing it at the stranger, who stood watching her with a disgusted expression on his rugged face, his hands placed negligently on his towel-clad hips, and not an ounce of fear in his attitude.

"Don't come near me, or I'll shoot!" Jackie's voice was ragged with fear, her eyes widened in terror, her hands trembling so much that the gun wavered with each shallow breath she took. She was riveted to the spot where she stood when every instinct made her want to back away from the tall intimidating figure who had invaded her sanctuary. Even the gun in her hands didn't make her feel secure, especially when the paralyzing thought reached her brain that it wasn't even loaded. Her eyes widened further at that realization, but then with lightning rapidity the thought followed that the stranger didn't *know* it wasn't loaded, and as long as he didn't, she could hold him off, perhaps force him to leave. The only argument against her conclusion was that the man wasn't showing the slightest sign that the gun made him nervous.

"Lady, will you put that thing down?" The request wasn't a request, it was an order. He sounded as though he were used to having his orders obeyed, too, and that thought triggered recognition. That voice! That tone! He was the man who had come to her door the previous night, demanding admittance, she realized. She felt an infinitesimal relaxation of her tension. The man had obviously sneaked back after she thought he had left and claimed what he protested were his rights. Had he spent the night there, then? she wondered.

The slight relaxation wasn't nearly enough to make her put the gun down. Whoever this intruder was, and for whatever reason he had intruded, he was still very much unwelcome, and she wanted him out of her cabin immediately.

"I will put this gun down the minute I see the back of your truck disappearing down that road away from here," she gritted out as forcefully as she could in her still wavering voice. "Now, get your clothes on and get out of here!"

"Ha! You'd like that, wouldn't you?" he said disgustedly, causing Jackie to think almost hysterically that that was the understatement of the year! It was *all* she would like at the moment. But then he went on.

"I told you last night that I had paid the rent on this cabin and that I have every right to be here. If anyone is going to be leaving, it's going to be you. I made the arrangements to stay here a year ago. I think that beats your two weeks by a long sight!"

Jackie could have screamed with frustration. Why wasn't the man afraid of the gun? How could he just stand there spouting his ridiculous litany about his *rights* when he had a gun trained on him, however waveringly, by a woman who was obviously one step away from mayhem? Didn't he have even a modicum of normal common sense? she wondered.

"I don't *care* about your stupid arrangements!" she shouted at him angrily. "The owner took my money, he said he had a cancellation, and I'm here! I'm not about to leave now, and I repeat, if you don't get out of here, I'll shoot you! Don't you understand plain English, you ass?"

The man's heavy well-shaped eyebrows came down in a frown of disapproval, his brown-flecked hazel eyes fixing her in a gleam of derision. "Watch your tongue, woman! I hate to hear a female use profanity, and besides"—a glint of amused arrogance appeared in the hazel eyes—"I may be a lot of things, but I'm not an ass. I got what I wanted last night, didn't I?"

The smug arrogance infuriated Jackie. The man was the limit! He might be courageous—as his disregard of the gun in her hands proved, unless he was just plain stupid, she amended her evaluation caustically—but he was a conceited boor along with it, and she fairly ached to prick the bubble of his conceit.

"How did you get in here?" she demanded, distracted by his reference to getting what he wanted. It could only mean he *had* spent the night in the cabin. The thought of him sleeping in the living room all night while she slept unknowing in the bedroom brought a shudder to her small frame. He could have done anything—raped her, robbed her, even killed her! The thought that he hadn't was only mildly reassuring.

"I came in through a window," he said with offhanded casualness, but then he fixed her with another of his disapproving glares. "You're a very foolish woman to be up here all alone. I could have been anyone and I could have done anything I wanted to you!" He echoed her own thoughts nastily. "What in the world possessed you to hole up here by yourself?"

He sounded genuinely puzzled beneath his disapproval, but his question merely goaded Jackie further. "That's none of your business!" she snapped. She gestured threateningly with the gun. "I'm not unprotected as you can see. And if you don't get out of here, you'll regret it. My patience is wearing very thin!"

The man grinned at that, disconcerting Jackie considerably. He had even white teeth, and the grin transformed his rugged masculine face into that of a charming sophisticate. For the first time she noted that he was really very attractive. He wasn't handsome in the way some men were, every feature perfect and symmetrical. His nose had obviously been broken at some time in the past, his jaw was too stubbornly masculine even through the white lather of the shaving soap that still adorned one side of his face, and his eyes were too disparagingly intelligent to ever soften with warmth, but the whole was virilely appealing in an uncomfortable sort of way. His perfect, tautly muscled physique contributed its share to that appeal, but it was too overtly, threateningly obtrusive at the moment for Jackie to appreciate its perfection. Jackie scowled at the man, who seemed to be enjoying their confrontation with such nasty appreciation. She preferred his temper to the amusement he was showing, though she couldn't have said why.

Suddenly he held out his hand toward her. "Give me that," he said with smiling tolerance. "Before you drop it and break your toe!" He took a step toward her, and Jackie backed away, her fear returning with full force. Her mind was wailing a useless litany of despair. Why wasn't he afraid? If he kept coming at her, what was she to do? she wondered. There were no bullets in the gun, and even if there had been, she wasn't certain she could shoot him. Could she perhaps throw it at him and dash around him to get to the door? She eyed his long arms and discarded the thought. He would have her in a minute.

Jackie's eyes darted helplessly around the room, searching for another weapon, anything she could use to stop the man, who was now stalking her deliberately as she continued to back away, but there was only so much room to back into. In the next second the matter was taken out of her hands as she felt her heels collide with one of her suitcases she had left carelessly on the floor the night before. Then she fell over backward with a yelp, the gun flying out of her hand to land against the wall on the other side of the bedroom, and she landed on her backside, her legs pulling the suitcase over on top of her, her head colliding with the wooden floor with a smarting thump.

For a moment she was slightly dazed, but not enough to shut out the sound of the man's obnoxious laughter as he reached down to give her a hand up. She slapped the hand away, glaring up into the laughing hazel eyes with fierce repugnance. "Don't touch me!" she snarled at him hatefully.

The man continued to grin at her, but he took his hand away and stood up, shrugging his broad shoulders in a gesture of negligible acceptance. "Suit yourself," he said with cheerful disconcern and turned his back on her to walk to where the gun lay on the floor.

Jackie was struggling to disentangle herself from the suitcase and was just getting to her feet when he walked back to her with the gun in his hand. She eyed it with wary caution, grateful that she *hadn't* loaded it once it was in his possession.

"This is a nice piece," the man said with casual interest. "I don't think it was damaged, but I'd have it looked over before it's fired again, if I were you."

Jackie stared disbelievingly as he offered it back to her. She looked from the gun to his face and back again, before reaching out a hand to take the weapon. When she looked at him once more he was smiling indulgently. "Why?" She said the one word rather helplessly, her bewilderment at his behavior apparent.

"Why am I giving it back to you?" he said with amused tolerance. "Because it isn't loaded," he explained reasonably, "the safety is on, and even if you've got some shells to put in it, I doubt if you know how."

Exasperated irritation sprang up anew and was apparent on Jackie's face as she glared at him, but he merely turned his back on her, chuckling disagreeably, and went to the door. "Get dressed," he ordered in his high-handed manner. "I'll finish shaving and get some clothes on myself. Then we'll sort out our differences in a civilized manner over some breakfast."

With that he was gone, and Jackie felt like hurling the useless gun after him. "Arrogant, conceited, male-chauvinist pig!" she muttered to herself as she flung off her robe and gown and searched for a pair of jeans and a top. Who *was* he anyway, with his stubborn determination to get his own way? If he thought he was going to chase her out of the cabin and take it for himself, then he'd better think again! She was definitely *not* leaving. *He* was! She liked it here. She knew instinctively that her time here would prove beneficial if she was only left in peace to enjoy it. Already, after only one evening and a night, she felt better than she had the entire past year, her wounds responding to the healing environment with a rapidity that was startling even to herself. And she was not about to let some self-important clod with a penchant for giving orders chase her away! she decided.

Jackie opened the bedroom door a cautious inch and peered out through the slit. The combination living room/kitchen was empty, which meant her unwelcome visitor was still in the bathroom. Relieved, she stepped through the door and pulled it closed behind her. The fireplace contained still-smoking embers, and she moved toward it to put a fresh log on and get the fire started again. The early morning air was chill, and she preferred the warmth of the wood fire to the electric heat.

She stopped short when she saw the sleeping bag stretched out in front of the fire, her anger returning to scorching pitch at the evidence that the stranger had indeed broken into the cabin in the middle of the night and spent the rest of it sleeping in that bag in front of *her* fire! The sheer nerve of that action infuriated her. Didn't he have any sense of decency? Did he think he was above the rules of common courtesy, not to mention the law of the land? He was nothing but a despicable burglar, that's what he was! she thought.

Jackie threw a log onto the fire after stepping contemptuously right in the middle of the sleeping bag to get to the wood supply. *Serve him right!* she thought with murderous intensity as she poked at the live embers, stirring them up to set the fresh log ablaze. She put on another log, then stood up to go to the kitchen and put on the coffee. As she ran water into the pot the sound of it made her uncomfortably aware that she needed to get into the bathroom and fast, and the thought that her unwelcome intruder was hogging it at the moment only increased her fury at him.

As if in answer to her thoughts, she heard the bathroom door open and she spun around to see the stranger emerge, freshly shaven, but still clad only in a towel. Her eyes raked his form scathingly, but if she had thought he would be moved by her disapproval, she was mistaken. He merely raised an eyebrow, nodded at her, and crossed the room to a bag that sat leaning against the end of the couch. He began to pull jeans and shirt out of the bag while Jackie watched, her expression thunderous.

"I'm going to get dressed now," he said with mild emphasis. "Are you going to watch?"

Jackie gasped in outrage, an outburst of incredulity hovering on her lips, when the man faced her, his expression calmly inquiring. She was about to let him *really* have the edge of her tongue when he shrugged and reached down to begin to unknot the towel.

"Oh!" Jackie gasped again, unable to believe the effrontery she was witnessing but convinced that the man would actually strip himself right there in front of her eyes if she didn't do something. She sped to the open bathroom door, crossed the threshhold, and slammed the door behind her, just catching the beginning of the hateful chuckle that was becoming so familiar already.

Once in the bathroom, Jackie remembered that she wanted to use its facilities, anyway, but the thought did nothing to soothe her feelings of abused insult. All the time she washed her face and brushed her teeth she was thinking furiously on how to get rid of the intruder. Of course, she couldn't throw him out physically herself, she knew. Any attempt at that was more likely to result in her own eviction. The bully probably wouldn't hesitate to toss her out on her ear, she thought with a curl of her lip, denoting her opinon of his gallantry, or rather the conspicuous lack of it. And she couldn't intimidate him into leaving. That had been proved beyond a shadow of a doubt. He had the hide of an elephant and the sensitivity of a snake! That left only an appeal to the landlord, which meant she would have to get in her car and drive all the way to Pinedale simply to claim what was her right, while the man who was the cause of it all took his ease in *her* cabin, while eating *her* food, no doubt!

Jackie combed her braid out with furious strokes, hurting her scalp in the process, but unaware of the resulting pain. Her hair framed her face in riotous curling waves when she was done, but she was aware only of the glint of fire sparking from her blue eyes and the heightened color of anger in her smooth cheeks. She felt no urge to put on makeup for the benefit of the man inhabiting her living room, and indeed she didn't need it. Her seething emotions provided a natural coloring that was far more attractive than any man-made artifices could have achieved.

Her first glimpse of the stranger was of his back as he stood at the stove, frying bacon—*her* bacon, she thought bitterly—when she emerged from the bathroom. At the sound of the door the man glanced at her over his shoulder, started to turn back to the stove, then returned his gaze to her again, an interested speculation crossing his features briefly. Jackie felt a slight chill at that look. She knew she was attractive. Enough men had paid her attention and complimented her on her looks that she couldn't be unaware of it. Until then, however, the aspect of her own appeal for a man hadn't filled her with anything but gratitude that nature had been kind to her and a certain amusement that men were so susceptible to outward appearances. She wondered if she might live to regret her blessings in that regard.

"Breakfast will be ready in a few minutes." The man spoke with casual aplomb, as though the two of them were old acquaintances rather than total inimicable strangers. "Would you set the table?"

Jackie controlled the instinctive protest that threatened to explode from her and took a deep breath instead. "Certainly," she said with sweet sarcasm. "I'm afraid we have only plain crockery, though. I would have brought my *best* china if I had known I was going to be allowed the *privilege* of entertaining!" The last was said with a snarl she couldn't control, but its effect was lost on the man she was addressing.

He glanced at her again, amusement gleaming from his eyes and twitching his mouth into a slight smile.

"And I'll bet your china is the best there is, ma'am," he said with mocking politeness, his eyes raking her form with appreciation. "You obviously have a lot of class." There was an unmistakable sexual note in his deep voice that effectively quelled Jackie's desire to engage in any more sparring with him.

The thing to do, she thought with grim determination, *is to get my purse, get out of here, and get the landlord before this madman decides he made a mistake by not raping me in my bed last night.* With that action in mind she began to move quietly toward the small table by the front door, where her purse rested, intending to snatch it up and get out the door before the man knew what she was about. He had turned his back to her again to flip the bacon, and she was grateful for the opportunity his action provided.

Her hand was descending to grab the purse when he spoke. "I took the liberty of extracting your car keys for the time being," he said quietly, the note of amusement just beneath the surface. "I thought you might try something like this, and we really should talk before you go haring down to fetch the sheriff. That *is* where you were going, I presume."

Jackie jumped, snatching her hand back as though it were burned. Then she rounded on the man in fury, caused both by the fear he had aroused when he spoke and despair at his anticipating what she had planned to do. "How *dare* you!" she spat at him angrily. "How *dare* you steal my keys!"

He shrugged, placing his hands on his hips and eyeing her rather wearily. "Look," he said with quiet authority, "I don't intend you any harm. I do intend to stay here. I've looked forward to this break for a long time and I know for a fact that there's not another place within miles where either one of us can stay. Now, will you cut out the outraged virgin act and get over here and set the table so we can eat? We'll work something out, I promise you.''

Jackie blinked at his tone, her anger dissipating in some miraculous way, replaced by an inexplicable compulsion to obey him. Where did he get that power to bend her to his will? she thought with abstracted bewilderment even as she crossed the distance back to the kitchen with hesitant steps. She was no pushover, but the man had such an air of authority. It was in his voice, his eyes and his stance as though he were used to unquestioning obedience and knew how to invoke it effortlessly. Certainly, *she* was obeying him, she thought with a return of her resentment as she got plates and cups from the cupboard and placed them on the table.

At least he hadn't gloated over his victory, she accorded him a grudging accolade. When he saw that she would do his bidding, he turned back to his cooking without a word and without the sneering triumph she had expected. That made her capitulation easier, if not acceptable, in her own mind.

When they were at last seated across from one another, the food he had prepared smelling deliciously appealing and looking as though it had been cooked by a cordon bleu chef, humble though a repast of bacon, eggs, and toast was, Jackie raised her eyes to his in one last, mutinously defiant gesture. He smiled at her then, crushing her defiance with devastating effectiveness. The smile was genuine, friendly, appealingly placatory. In short, irresistible. Jackie flushed at her own reaction to that smile. It had stirred something in her she thought was lost for good when Matt died—a short, sharp stab of desire. She dropped her eyes in confusion and picked up her fork.

They ate in silence, apart from polite requests to pass this or that. Jackie was shaken by her reaction to this stranger. She knew nothing about him. For all she knew, he could be the most despicable man alive. Then why didn't she feel repulsed by him? she asked herself with wry incomprehension. Of course, there were charming con men all over the world who had a gift for lulling their victims to their own destruction. But somehow—she glanced up from underneath her lashes to look at the face of the man across from her— she couldn't picture him as a con man. There was integrity in that face, intelligence in those eyes. Whatever he was, she felt certain, without knowing how she knew, that he was trustworthy. Rude, overbearing, arrogant, highhanded, but trustworthy.

Jackie stifled the giggle that bubbled up inside her at her thoughts, a giggle inspired partly by the remnants of the near hysteria she had experienced earlier and relief that she could feel safe again.

"You make good coffee." The compliment was delivered as a statement, not an attempt to gain her favor, she felt certain. Its tone was too matter-of-fact.

"Thank you," she responded with dry politeness. "Your food is delicious," she added belatedly, and without the ease with which she would normally have dispatched a sincere observation. It felt ridiculous to be exchanging those polite pleasantries under the circumstances.

He placed his elbows on the table, the coffee cup between his large capable, though somehow sensitive-looking hands. Jackie noted that his nails were shaped neatly and were clean. Obviously, he didn't work with them unless by choice, she thought. She raised her eyes from his hands to his face and saw that he was watching her with an intent appraisal that was discomfitting in its thoroughness. She felt like a bug under a microscope.

"Are you ready to talk now—reasonably?" The brusque tone was all business, and Jackie responded in kind.

"Quite ready," she said with cold formality. "Although I don't see that there's much to talk about, really. I fail to see where you have a leg to stand on. You're guilty of breaking and entering, trespassing..." She shrugged as though her point were made. "Regardless of whether you feel you have a right to be here, that doesn't excuse your behavior. Don't you have any respect for the law?"

The man smiled a slow smile that brought a charm to his face Jackie would have preferred not to notice. His mouth was firm, yet sensuously tender, and his eyes seemed to light with the smile, their peculiar intensity piercing her outward composure. "Oh, I think I do," he replied with soft amusement. He reached into an upper pocket and withdrew a piece of paper, then offered it to her. Jackie took it reluctantly.

It was a receipt from John Reardon for a month's stay at the cabin. Jackie firmed her lips in an uncon-

scious gesture of challenge. She was torn between relief at the undeniable evidence that the man across
from her was not a crook, but rather an honest man
who felt he had been cheated, and chagrin at the same
evidence, which indicated he had a legitimate right to
dispute her claim to the cabin.

Jackie gave the man—she knew his name now, as it
was printed on the piece of paper in awkward letter-
ing, Adam Clarke—an unflinching look and rose to
her feet to go and get her purse. In a moment, she
came back and handed him an identical sheet of
paper—her receipt for a three-month stay. He took it,
looked at it, his eyes lingering on her name then
handed it back to her with a shrug. There was a challenging look in his eyes as well, and Jackie had the
uncomfortable feeling that in the battle that was now
about to take place, he would prove the stronger. But
not if she could help it. Her creative imagination had
to be good for something against his brawn, she
thought.

"Checkmate!" His humorous comment failed to
elicit any matching amusement on Jackie's part, if
that had been his intention.

"Oh, I don't think so," she said firmly. "After all, I
was here first. And as I believe I commented to you
last night, possession is still nine tenths of the law."
She resumed her seat at the table, folded her hands
under her chin, and faced him squarely, making the
effort to hold his gaze with her own.

"Do you know very much about the law, Miss...
Mrs?..." he questioned gently, "... er, Roth, isn't
it?"

"It's *Mrs.* Roth," she emphasized with a slight catch in her voice, then realized she didn't have her wedding ring on when she saw him looking at her hand. A few months after Matt's death she had taken it off and put it away at Dr. Chelski's suggestion. It had become a constant reminder of her pain, and Dr. Chelski had only proposed the gesture as a temporary measure to enable her time to adjust. But she had never put it back on, because at each inclination to do so, after she had taken it out, the pain had been there again. She thought now she could probably wear it again without experiencing that pain, but she was in such a hurry when she left, she had forgotten to bring it.

Jackie debated with herself briefly about explaining her marital status to the stranger. It was none of his business, of course, but somehow, with his clear penetrating eyes upon her, she found herself saying the words seemingly without volition. "I'm a widow...." Her voice trailed away, and she had to drop her eyes at the sudden compassion she saw in his. She hadn't told him to evoke pity, damn it! she thought angrily. She didn't know why she had told him at all. She just wanted to get rid of him. That was all she knew for certain, she told herself with a certain degree of desperation.

"May I call you Jacqueline?" His response took her by surprise, and she didn't know what to say. She didn't *want* any such intimacy as to be on a first-name basis with him implied, even if Jacqueline did sound so formal to her own ears. She had been used to Jackie for so long, as so few people called her Jacqueline, and then only strangers, but then he *was* a stranger, wasn't he? she remembered with a slight sense of shock. Why had she begun to feel that she knew him, perhaps could *like* him? she wondered.

"I don't care what you call me," she said, impatience in her voice. "I would just like you to leave, and then we won't have to worry about it, will we?"

Adam Clarke sat back in his chair, one arm thrown over the back in a casual pose, and shook his head with slow, thoughtful deliberation. "I can't do that," he said quietly.

"Can't, or won't?" Jackie said with exasperated sharpness. "*Why* can't you, or won't you?" There was an unconscious plea for cooperation in her blue eyes that caught his attention, and for a moment Jackie thought he was going to weaken, but only for a moment. Then he stood and picked up his cup to go to the counter for more coffee.

"I've just bought a house in Missoula, Montana," he said as he turned back to face her. "It's being redecorated. I planned this trip to coincide with the work and gave up my apartment the day I left to come here—yesterday." He took a sip of the coffee and watched her reaction over the rim of the cup. "So you see, I have nowhere to go right now."

Jackie frowned at him, trying to ascertain the truth of his statements. "But there must be other places around here where you can stay," she pleaded desperately. "It shouldn't be too hard to find another cabin."

One eyebrow arched up, and he gave her a skeptical look from eyes suddenly grown cool with that piercing look of intelligent perception she found so uncomfortable to endure. "You think so?" he said mockingly. "In hunting season?"

Jackie bit her lip with vexation. She had forgotten that deer hunters from all over the country gathered here at this time of year. He was probably perfectly correct in assuming that any decent accommodations within miles had been booked months previously. She hardened her heart and challenged him again. "How do you suppose this mix-up occurred?" she said suspiciously. "Mr. Reardon said he had a cancellation. I assume it could only have been yours. Now you turn up here and want to renege on that cancellation, expecting me to clear out, and it just isn't fair! I won't do it!"

She had clenched her hands into fists unconsciously, and Adam Clarke glanced at her belligerent gesture with a small smile of male tolerance. "Who said anything about your clearing out?" he said mildly.

Jackie's eyes widened in astonishment, and her tone was soft with hope as she said, "You mean *you'll* leave?"

He shook his head with mocking firmness. "Not at all," he said with undisguised determination. "I meant we could *share* the cabin."

Jackie's mouth dropped open for a moment, and her eyes reflected her shock. "You're out of your mind!" she protested finally, sparks of outrage snapping from her eyes as she jumped to her feet and gripped the back of her chair tightly. "I'm not about to share this cabin with you or anyone else!"

Clarke shrugged and set his coffee cup down. "Then I guess you will have to leave," he said matter-of-factly, "because I'm sure as hell not!"

Jackie had the crazy impression of watching an immovable rock open its mouth to speak those words. This man meant what he said, and something about him convinced her that nothing she could do or say would change his mind. She wanted to hit him for his stubborn invincibility, strike out at him for disrupting what had promised to be a delightful, productive interlude in her life—one she needed and was certainly not going to give up without a fight!

"We'll see about that," she promised him grimly. "Give me my keys!"

Adam Clarke eyed her up and down for a moment, then reached into his pants pocket and drew out her keys, holding them up for her to come and get them from him with a hateful smile on his mocking lips.

"Come and get them," he said with soft invitation.

Jackie stomped across the room and snatched them from his hand. "I'm going into Pinedale to see John Reardon," she said with a promise of retribution in her tone. "You'd better pack up, because when I get back with him, you're going to be thrown out on your ear, *Mr.* Clarke!" she sneered.

His eyes gleamed, and Adam Clarke barely contained a laugh. "Call me Adam, Jack," he said in a tone of amused camaraderie, shocking her into stillness with his use of the name Matt had always called her. "I have the feeling we might as well dispense with formality and treat one another like two old hunting buddies. After all, we're going to be living together for the next month."

With that he sidestepped away from her and returned to the table, beginning to clear away the breakfast dishes. Jackie stood in frustrated rage for another bare second before she flung away to get her coat and purse and storm out the door of the cabin to find her car to drive to Pinedale.

All the way into town she kept hearing the cheerful sound of Adam Clarke's whistling as he cleared the dishes—hearing it, and hating it, and vowing to change his tune just as soon as she could get John Reardon back with her to help her do it.

Chapter Four

The small cheerful café was packed with citizens of Pinedale who wanted to get in out of the rain and exchange a bit of gossip with their neighbors before going back to whatever chores they could find to occupy themselves with on a day unfit for outdoor activity. Jackie sat at a small table in a corner, drinking coffee, her discouragement plain on her face and in her slumped posture. She was remembering her interview with Mrs. Reardon, and her thoughts were gloomy to say the least.

Mr. Reardon was away on a visit to his elderly mother in Cheyenne, so Jackie had to be satisfied with talking to Mrs. Reardon, a small, peppery woman who talked so fast and listened so haphazardly that it was like battling one's way through a hurricane of words to get any satisfaction. And as it turned out, there was little satisfaction to be had.

Jackie determined on the way into Pinedale that she would first ask if there were any other cabins to rent in the area. If there was even one, perhaps she could have John Reardon talk Adam Clarke into taking it and leaving her in peace. And if there wasn't, then she would just have to ask Mr. Reardon to come back with her and insist that Adam leave. If Mr. Reardon would—and if Adam would! She was not at all sure that Mr. Reardon would even be able to dislodge her unwelcome intruder from his attachment to her cabin, but it was worth a chance.

Yet Mr. Reardon wasn't there, and when Jackie made her inquiry to Mrs. Reardon, the woman immediately launched into a tirade about how "city folks"—obviously meaning Jackie—were always finding something to complain about when the cabin was as nice a place as one could find in the whole state of Wyoming. The older woman obviously thought Jackie was dissatisfied with the place, and Jackie tried to amend her interpretation, but to no avail. The woman pointed out triumphantly that the rent was nonrefundable.

After emitting a sigh of frustration, Jackie switched tactics. She asked about the cancellation, and whether Mr. Clarke had phoned in his cancellation personally, whereupon Mrs. Reardon asked suspiciously how Jackie knew that *Judge* Clarke was the one who had rented the place previously. Somehow, in the midst of her shock at hearing Adam Clarke referred to as *Judge* Clarke, Jackie managed to mumble something incoherent about Mr. Reardon mentioning the matter.

Relaxing somewhat, Mrs. Reardon then allowed that no, Judge Clarke hadn't made the call, his secretary had. It had been a real shocker to hear it, too, Judge Clarke being one of their best customers for years past. She hoped he wasn't sick, because a nicer man never lived, and it was a real pity he hadn't been able to take his yearly vacation. The poor man needed it so, working as hard as he did. And on and on and on... Mrs. Reardon was obviously a fan of Adam's, and Jackie's hopes of soliciting help in evicting him from the cabin grew dimmer with each word of praise that fell gushingly from Mrs. Reardon's lips. That, coupled with the fact that Mrs. Reardon was outraged at what she perceived to be Jackie's disapproval of the cabin, proved to be more than Jackie could overcome. She solicited the information that Mr. Reardon wouldn't be returning for a week or more, depending upon whether his poor, dear mother recovered quickly. That was said with such hypocritical malice toward the absent mother-in-law that Jackie felt it was a good thing Mr. Reardon had gone alone, or his wife might have hampered his mother's recovery permanently.

Jackie sat brooding over her coffee, wondering what on earth she was supposed to do now. Without Mr. Reardon's support there was no hope of getting rid of Adam. And there was nowhere for Jackie to go, Mrs. Reardon having been adamant that there wasn't a place to be had this side of Cheyenne. Jackie didn't want to leave the area, anyway. Damn it, she liked it here! she thought. But she couldn't go back and share that cabin with Adam Clarke. It was out of the question, she knew.

The coffee had gone cold, and Jackie ordered another cup, not knowing what else to do with herself. She was well and truly stuck for a solution to her problem. She didn't even know where she was to spend the night, much less the next three months.

Jackie was raising the cup to her lips when she saw a tall familiar figure enter the café, her eyes widening in disbelief. What was Adam doing here? Had he changed his mind and decided to be decent about the whole thing? Fat chance, she thought disgustedly as he wound his way through the tables to reach her side. He looked anything but conciliatory as he took the seat across from her and motioned for the waitress to bring him coffee.

"Make yourself at home," Jackie said disagreeably. "You have a remarkable facility for that, don't you?"

Adam smiled at her with smug complacence, not answering, then turned the full beam of his charm on the waitress, who was hurrying to bring him his coffee. "Hello, Annie," he said in warm fullsome tones that had the effect of reducing the middle-aged waitress to a state of giggling confusion.

"Hello, Judge," said Annie, gushing every bit as disgustingly as Mrs. Reardon had, Jackie noted with a jaundiced eye. "I'm glad to see you back. Will you be staying long this time?"

Adam cast a glance of mischievous conspiracy at Jackie, who felt a strong urge to kick him under the table. "I plan to spend every possible moment I can spare here, Annie," he answered with innocent enthusiasm. "You know how I love it here."

Annie fairly beamed at Adam, seemingly overjoyed at this information, while Jackie groaned inwardly and gritted her teeth with hostility. Then Annie turned her attention to Jackie, apparently expecting an introduction and avidly curious as to whom the Judge had with him. Jackie stiffened somewhat, at a loss as to what to say. She didn't get the chance to say anything, however, as Adam smoothly performed the introduction.

"Annie, I'd like you to meet Jacqueline Roth." Then he dropped a bombshell that had Jackie blinking at him in shock. "My fiancée," he said simply, his eyes glinting with the dare that Jackie contradict him.

Jackie was about to do just that as soon as she recovered her equilibrium in the face of his colossal nerve, but Annie didn't give her a chance.

"Ohhh...." Annie stared at Jackie as though it were Queen Elizabeth sitting there. "You lucky, lucky thing, you," she breathed softly, her tone making it clear that Jackie had been accorded an honor no mere mortal had a right to expect.

Infuriated, Jackie opened her mouth to set both of them straight once and for all when a man two tables away called to Annie. "Hey, Annie, I need a refill. Move it, will you!"

Annie beamed a wavering smile at Adam and Jackie, and Jackie was surprised to see that there were tears shimmering in her faded blue eyes. "Congratulations!" she said wholeheartedly, and then she was gone to take care of her impatient customer, and Jackie was left to face an amused Adam, whose expression made it evident he knew exactly what Jackie had wanted to say.

"Don't say a word," he ordered softly, and then he chuckled at the furious defiance in Jackie's eyes. "Not unless you want everyone in this small town to think you'll be living with me without benefit of any commitment at all."

Words sputtered on Jackie's lips, but Adam cut them off. "Face it," he said with authority. "You didn't get anywhere with Reardon, I'm sure. You haven't got anywhere to go except the cabin, I'm sure of that as well." He spread his hands in a gesture of finality. "What choice have you got except to return with me and make the best of it?"

Jackie scorched him with a look. "I'd rather sleep in the car and freeze to death!" she said with melodramatic fury.

Adam shook his head at her chidingly. "Why? I'm a good companion if you'll give me a chance. And if it's your virtue you're worried about, don't give it a thought. I assure you, I won't." There was laughter behind his last remark, but then he relented when Jackie made to stand up and leave him. He reached over and grasped her hand to keep her where she was. "Seriously," he said with a suitably serious tone to match the word "I feel guilty about disrupting your plans and I promise I won't make a nuisance of myself if you'll come back with me. We probably won't even see much of each other. I plan to go out hunting every day that the weather's suitable."

Jackie eyed him with wary disgust. "I might have known you'd be a hunter," she said with scathing dislike. "Do you take pleasure in killing a helpless deer? I don't see how you can stand to shoot one when they look at you with those wonderful brown eyes."

She was playing for time, unaccountably tempted by Adam's promise to leave her alone if she went back to the cabin with him, but unable as yet to give in to that temptation. It was a totally new quandary for her. She had been reared with strict notions about the proprieties between men and women, and she knew that her parents, and especially her grandparents, would have been shocked to the core at her even entertaining the idea of sharing accommodations with Adam. But would Matt have been shocked? She thought not. Matt had had a practical, commonsense approach to life that left little room for attention to cultural taboos he found ridiculous. He had had his own morality, and it was a strict one, yet it was far removed from mere surface appearances.

What it boiled down to, really, she mused with cool thoughtfulness, was whether she trusted Adam Clarke to keep his word...and his distance. He had not responded to her gibe about his hunting, seeming to be aware that she was searching for straws—distractions—to avoid the decision she was going to have to make. Jackie glanced down at their hands. Adam had not yet released her, and the strength and warmth of his large hand on hers was disturbingly pleasant. That brought another worry to mind as she remembered her reaction to his smile earlier in the day when they had sat down together to eat breakfast. What if it wasn't Adam's honor she had to worry about? What if it was her own? She was lonely. At times she fairly ached to feel Matt's arms around her again, holding her close and filling her with the heady sexual excitement she had come to desire as strongly as he had during the years of their marriage. She hadn't thought it possible that anyone else could evoke those feelings, but in Adam Clarke she sensed not only the possibility, but almost a certainty that she could want him if she let herself. Surely that in itself was reason enough to back away from the arrangement he was proposing. Or was it? she wondered.

Jackie shocked herself with the thought. She never thought of herself as the type to have an affair, yet she was thirty years old, lonely, self-sufficient enough to survive on her own, but needed the simple human sustenance of another's touch. Not without the requisite caring, she decided suddenly, relieved to find herself returning to safer ground. The possibility of an affair was not set aside as unthinkable, as it would have been such a short time ago in the past, but she knew there would have to be some sort of commitment to make it possible—some very real emotion behind the act to make it justifiable. She lifted her eyes to Adam's to find him watching the play of emotions cross her face with intense interest, and she hoped fervently that he was not one of the few people in the world blessed with ESP.

"We would have to have some firm ground rules," she said hesitantly, and felt his hand relax its tension on her own. There was approval in his eyes, she noted with a strange sense of pleasure in the realization. How odd that it should give her pleasure to evoke that approval when only seconds before, she would have said she didn't give a damn for what he thought, she mused.

"Yes, of course," he said softly. And then his manner returned to the brusque, businesslike authority she found so contradictorily reassuring, yet at the same time disappointing. She shook herself mentally, wondering with wry disgust what it was she *did* want from him. Whatever it was, she had better decide soon if she hoped to have any chance of imposing her own will on their relationship. A man like Adam was capable of dominating everyone around him if they let him get away with it. She would have to make sure she didn't.

"You keep the bedroom," he was saying now. "I'll continue to sleep in front of the fire."

Jackie bristled at his suggestion that there might have been any question that she would keep the bedroom. A picture of his long frame interposed itself hard on the heels of her self-righteous possessiveness over the bedroom, however, and she found herself thinking how unfair it was to subject him to the hard floor when she was short enough to fit comfortably on the couch, as she had done when she had visited the cabin with her parents.

"I can sleep on the couch," she said with tart umbrage at his taking over their sleeping arrangements. He wasn't to know her sharpness was due more to her instinctive realization that he would be more likely to accept her suggestion if he thought it came from irritation than from a desire for his comfort. Besides, she didn't want him to know she was concerned for his comfort. In any case, he swept her suggestion aside.

"You'll sleep in the bedroom," he declared uncompromisingly, and Jackie thought with exasperation that if this were what he meant by setting the ground rules, it was clear he meant to set them, and she was going to be left to follow them. "We'll share the cooking and cleaning duties," he went on as though he were dictating a note to a secretary. "Anything else that comes up, we'll tackle on a one-on-one basis."

"What?" Jackie was startled by his way of putting the last statement, then embarrassed by the sly grin he gave her that told her she had a dirty mind.

"I mean," he said with innocent reasonableness, "that each time any matter arises where there's a conflict, we'll settle it then and there. We can't anticipate *everything* can we?"

Jackie's cheeks were flushed pink with embarrassment at her innocent provocativeness and anger at his put-down. If it *was* a put-down, she thought with frustrated bewilderment as she nodded as coolly as possible to signify she understood his words.

"Fine," he said with expansive satisfaction. "Then what do you say we get back there and begin our life together?" There was a wicked taunting in his voice that Jackie refused to react to. It was plain that Adam enjoyed setting her up for his perverse humor, and the best way to handle that was simply not to react at all.

He stood up and stretched his powerful body before reaching down a hand to help her up. Jackie would have liked to refuse the offer, but she caught Annie's eyes on them, so she smiled faintly and placed her hand in Adam's. "Never let it be said I killed the joy of vicarious romance," she muttered witheringly as Adam pulled her up beside him.

His eyes found Annie, and he winked at the waitress before pulling Jackie close to his side and wrapping an arm around her waist. "Good girl," he whispered into her ear with disturbing effects on her senses. "Annie deserves a little joy in her life, vicarious or not. It's kind of you to consider her feelings."

Jackie couldn't tell if he was serious or not, and she had all she could handle just enduring the physical proximity of a man who seemed unaware that his touch was evoking all the sensuality Jackie had suppressed for a year and a half. She could only wonder with a sense of fatalism what she had let herself in for by agreeing to live with Adam. The only light at the end of the tunnel was the fact that he had only signed on at the cabin for a month. Surely she could damp down her reactions for that long.

Once outside, Jackie remembered Adam's huge appetite at breakfast that morning and she stopped and pointed at a nearby grocer. "Go buy yourself some food before you come home, Adam Clarke. If you think I'm going to feed a frame like yours on my budget, you're very much mistaken. I'll see you at the cabin!"

She heard his inevitable chuckle as she turned away and started for her car, her back straight and her step firmly independent. She found it uncommonly strange that the chuckle sounded deeply, masculinely attractive when earlier it had grated on her nerves like chalk on a blackboard, but she thrust the thought away from her as she climbed in her car and gunned it away from the curb in a burst of speed that echoed her need to get away from Adam's imposing presence for a while. It was only after she had traveled several miles that she remembered she had spoken to him like a wife, rather than like the strangers they were, telling him to get food before he came *home*, for heaven's sake! Jackie winced visibly at the recollection and determined that she would have to watch herself very closely where Adam Clarke was concerned. It would be far too easy to fall into a pattern of domesticity with him that could well prove hard to break when it came time to separate. She refused to speculate on why the thought of separation from him had already the power to bring a sense of bleak loneliness in its path. She would cope, she told herself firmly. She had before and she would again. Of course she would, damn it! She was becoming very, very good at coping, she realized.

Chapter Five

Adam returned to the cabin just as Jackie was finishing the last of her unpacking. She had debated only briefly about the advisability of signaling her intention to stay in such an unequivocable manner, then decided that if she was in for a penny, she might as well be in for a pound. After she filled the small bedroom closet and rickety bureau drawers with her clothes, she was able to greet Adam's return in a mood of hostess greeting a guest, a mood that lasted all of five minutes before Adam had effectively turned the tables on her.

He started the process by carting in what looked to be a full ton of food to Jackie's startled eyes, and she wondered where on earth he would find the storage space to dispose of it. She had pretty well filled the limited cupboard area and the small refrigerator herself the previous day. However, with an economy of motion that told her he was no stranger to this particular kitchen, and with a seeming genius for organization, he soon had the food neatly packed away and was turning his hand to cleaning the bathroom, which, contrary to her experience with Matt, he had not left in all that much of a mess in the first place.

While he was busy Jackie made a show of arranging a small table to fit her writing needs, placing her typewriter just so on the edge of it and stacking a generous amount of paper where it was handy to her reach. She wanted to stake her claim to this small section of the cabin from the beginning, intending to make it very clear to Adam that this was a working holiday for her and that she would tolerate no interference from her unwelcome companion.

It was therefore disconcerting when, upon finishing his bathroom chores, Adam reentered the living room, glanced at the neat working space, fixed her with one of his piercing looks, and said, "You're a writer?"

"Yes." Jackie, taken aback by his quick perception—after all, simply the possession of a typewriter and paper could have placed her in any number of categories other than writer—was about to recover her tongue and read him the riot act about the peace and privacy she required, when he took the wind out of her sails.

"Perfect," he said, as though her profession were a direct result of *his* planning. "You can write all day while I'm out hunting. I see now why you came here in the first place." There was satisfaction in his observation, as though he had disposed of a mystery that had been bothering him, and then he proceeded to both flabbergast her and enrage her in one fell blow, with the added irritation that she was left without a suitable reply to put him down. "You won't write at night, though, will you." It was not a question, or a request. It was a laying down of the law. "I hear enough typewriters pounding all day the rest of the year not to want to hear that while I'm here." He fixed her with one of his charming smiles that took the breath out of the hot retort hovering on her lips. "Besides, you look like the type who would work herself to death if you didn't have someone drawing a line somewhere. I guess it will be up to me to do that for you while we're together."

And what was she supposed to reply to that? Jackie fumed silently as she turned away to hide her confusion at the quick shaft of pleasure she had felt while hearing the possessive, caretaking note in his voice. Since Matt's death there had been no one to *care* whether she worked herself too hard.

But she was not at all sure she liked having Adam Clarke place himself in the position of her watchdog so easily and confidently, and she was certain she didn't like her pleasurable response to his dominance. A little shiver of warning went down her spine when she reflected that it was only their first day together, and already she was accepting his orders meekly in a throwback to the days when all a man had to do was tell a woman to jump, and she would ask "How high?"

In reaction to her dismay at her own weakness she proceeded to pick a fight with Adam at the first opportunity. It came with astonishing speed.

"I'll need half of the drawers in your bedroom," he announced in his most irritating dominant tone. "I have to have somewhere to put my clothes."

Jackie immediately bristled. "You can keep them in your bag!" she retorted, adopting a challenging stance with hands on her hips. "If you think I'm going to have you coming into my bedroom at all hours, rummaging through the drawers like a bull in a china shop, you're mistaken! The bedroom is off limits as far as you're concerned!"

Adam had been bending over his duffel bag, drawing the strings together tightly, preparatory to lifting it to his shoulder. When he turned his head to look at her, the light in his eyes made Jackie take an involuntary step backward. He looked like a predatory animal who had just sighted his dinner and was plotting strategy in order to capture it. He straightened up and swung the heavy bag over his shoulder, then walked to within two steps of where Jackie stood forcing herself to hold her ground.

"Jack, let's get one thing straight here and now," he said softly, his tone all the more dangerous for its quiet implacability. "If I wanted to, I could take you by force any time I damn well pleased." His eyes raked her slight form meaningfully, and Jackie, forced into a comparison of their relative physical strengths, saw his point with the same force she had experienced only that morning when finding him in her bathroom. She swallowed nervously, but managed to hold his eyes with her own. "That's what's worrying you, I presume," he went on with only a slight questioning tone in his voice. "The thing you need to understand is that I've never taken a woman by force in my life, and I don't intend to break the pattern with you." Jackie felt a little stung by the phrasing of his statement. He made it sound as though she weren't *worth* breaking his lifelong habit for. There was no time to feel more than a passing resentment, however, as he continued.

"We can't live together for a month without trust," he was saying emphatically. "And we can't live together without some relaxation of the normal rules that would govern a situation of this kind...." There was humor in his next words, which brought a tiny relaxation to the tension Jackie was laboring under. "If there *are* any other situations of this kind or ever have been." But then he made his point. "And that includes my use of the drawers in the bedroom. I'll be as considerate as I can, but you're going to have to bend those rigid little morals of yours slightly on occasion if we're going to make this work."

Jackie opened her mouth to take umbrage to his classifying of her morals as little and rigid, but he cut her off. "And you'd better do something about that temper of yours, as well. I don't mind a good scrap now and then myself, but I'll be damned if I'll live with a constant barrage from that charming mouth of yours. Haven't you learned yet to put it to better use?" With that he grasped her chin in his large hand and lowered his lips to hers. "Like this?" he muttered under his breath before scorching her mouth with a short devastating demonstration of his meaning.

Jackie was shocked into immobility, and the kiss was so brief, there wasn't time to protest before he had raised his head, his eyes laughing into hers at her speechlessness. "There," he said with gentle mockery. "Now, isn't that just like a man? He assures a woman of his honest intentions in one breath and kisses her speechless with the next.'' He straightened and shifted the bag on his shoulder, a devilish grin on his lips. ''There's no accounting for us, is there?'' And with that he turned away and strode to the door of the bedroom, whistling a cheerful tune as though nothing had happened to rock Jackie's world on its pinions. She stood where she was, grateful to have a few moments in which to collect her whirling thoughts and quieten the senses Adåm had woken with such devastating impact in one brief, careless moment of devilment.

She raised a hand to her trembling lips, meaning to wipe away the kiss that had shaken her to the core, and instead traced her mouth almost reverently, awed by how such brief contact of one mouth against another could have such far-reaching consequences. An image of Matt entered her mind, bringing with it a sudden stab of guilt at what she considered a betrayal of his memory, but then it was gone. Matt would never have wanted her to chain herself to his ghost, refusing to live her life out of some misguided notion of loyalty to him, just as she would never have expected him to eschew the happiness of finding someone to take her place if *she* had been the one who died.

Jackie shook her head with a helpless gesture of bewilderment. Why was she standing here thinking such thoughts when all Adam had done was kiss her? she asked herself. He hadn't meant anything by it, she was certain, unless it was simply to shake her up, make her more amenable to his demands that she cooperate with him in making their cohabitation workable. And here she was spinning dreams of turning their short association into something permanent! How ridiculous could one get?

Angry with herself, Jackie grabbed up her jacket and went to the front door, meaning to walk off her nervous disquiet and return to the cabin in a frame of mind more conducive to making life with Adam possible. She had her hand on the knob when he emerged from the bedroom and frowned at seeing her obviously intending to leave. "I'm going for a walk," she said hastily, forestalling the question she saw in his eyes. "I need some exercise." She pulled open the door and was across the threshold before he could comment, slamming the door behind her.

She was only a few paces away when she heard the door opening, and she tensed at the expectation of hearing him protest, though why he should, she didn't know. But all he said was, "Be careful, Jack." And his tone was quietly thoughtful, as though he had matters of more import on his mind. "Watch where you're going, so you don't get lost."

Jackie nodded briefly, not bothering to turn to face him, and strode off across the clearing toward the woods as though she had an urgent appointment to keep. And indeed she did—an appointment to come to terms with how Adam Clarke made her senses come alive, made long-suppressed longings wake up to haunt her, made silly daydreams spin inside her head. All of those things would have to be dealt with if she was going to get through the next few weeks heartwhole, self-respect intact. The question was, how did she accomplish the task she was setting herself? How did one turn off such feelings once they were aroused? she wondered. She had no experience to help her, never having been faced with such a situation before. She thought wryly that maybe it was her turn to go through what was popularly known as an unrequited love affair, but it was not a very good time in her life to have to play catch up. She could have dealt with something like that much more easily had she not already been subjected to the pain of losing Matt.

It was not long before the soothing effect of her surroundings quieted her anxieties and took her mind off Adam. She walked on pine needles made soft and damp by the earlier rain, smelled the scents of the forest, clean and fresh as only nature could be, and heard the soft rustlings of birds and small animals as they went about their business oblivious of her intrusion. A small brook rippled by the path she had taken, and Jackie followed it, unconsciously abiding by Adam's instructions that she not get lost. The brook would serve as her guide when she was ready to return to the cabin.

At length she reached a small open area where the brook widened into a pool and a large rock offered seating. It was a delightful spot, and Jackie sat to rest her legs and let the peace of the clearing settle into her soul. The rock was large enough to let her lean back on her elbows, and she did so, lifting her face to the few rays of sun that cut through the clouds above her. A sigh of contentment left her lips, and she thought she would have liked to stay there forever, but, of course, she couldn't. There was work on her novel to be done back at the cabin... and there was Adam.

With her senses lulled by her surroundings, Jackie was able to reflect more calmly on what had happened, chiding herself for her earlier upset. What was in a kiss, after all? Adam was attractive, yes. He had the power to stir her physically, but perhaps there were scores of men who could do that, though she cast a skeptical inner eye on that observation, feeling she might be going just a little too far in her efforts to justify her reaction to Adam, and explain it away into nothingness. But even if he was in a class by himself, what of it? she thought philosophically as she sat up to rest her chin on her knee. There was more to life and relationships than sex. Just because a man's touch could turn her to jelly didn't mean they were made for each other. She barely knew Adam. There was every chance that when she *got* to know him, she would find he didn't appeal to her in any other way than the physical.

And what about Adam's part in all this? she scolded herself mercilessly. Apart from the kiss, he had given no indication that he was interested in her as a woman, and even the kiss had been given more in the way of a punishment than a seduction. Wasn't she jumping the gun a little by even *speculating* on developing a relationship with Adam? He might even be married! The thought widened her eyes and caught her breath in her throat. She was annoyed by the relief she felt when she remembered that he would hardly have announced that the two of them were engaged if he was already married. Surely the townspeople—

Annie, in fact—would have known had he been married and raised an eyebrow at his suddenly introducing a fiancée!

Suddenly Jackie was tired of wrestling with the matter. It was much too soon to be agonizing over something that had no basis in reality. She and Adam Clarke were strangers, thrown together by fate for one short month out of their lives, and no doubt destined to part forever at the end of that month. What was the point in making more of the situation than was there? She would take things as they came from then on, refusing to let Adam Clarke dominate her thoughts to the exclusion of everything else again.

With that decision made she jumped up and started back to the cabin, determinedly concentrating on the beauty around her instead of thoughts of Adam, and succeeding to the extent that when she broke through the woods into the clearing surrounding her temporary abode, she was smiling and humming and in a much better temper than when she had set out.

Adam caught her mood at once, and the two of them managed to construct a dinner of steaks, salad, and wine without once resorting to a cross word or even an annoyed look. Later they sat before the fire, content and drowsy from the food and the atmosphere of peaceful cheer created by the flames. For a long while there seemed no necessity to talk, but eventually Jackie's curiosity got the better of her.

"Aren't you a little young to be a judge?" she asked with drowsy interest. "I thought judges were white-haired and wrinkled—Solomon's heirs, or something like that."

Out of the corner of her eye Jackie discovered that when Adam smiled, as he was now in reaction to her question, he had an endearing little crease at the corner of his mouth that was extraordinarily kissable. Jumbled up with that recognition was the knowledge that her question had perhaps not been phrased in as tactful a manner as she was wont to display, but then she was tired, she excused herself lamely.

"Did you ever consider that the people of Montana may be able to recognize real talent when they see it, even when it's embodied in a relative youngster like me?" he drawled tongue in cheek, and then added sotto voce, "Unlike some people I could mention."

Jackie flushed a little in embarrassment and rising temper at his conceit, but even as her reaction was gaining steam, she realized there was a note of self-mockery in his reply that denied her evaluation. Further, she wondered if he might be playing his perverse game of trying to get a rise out of her so he could pounce on her again when and if he succeeded. The thought sparked a desire to beat him to the punch. She turned and smiled sweetly at him, her blue eyes as guileless as a babe's.

"Are you saying you *do* equate your talents with Solomon's?" she asked innocently.

Adam met her look and her question with a gleam of combat in his eyes and a twitching quirk to his mouth. "Ummm, no..." he said with lazy consideration. "It wouldn't be a fair comparison. Ethics were a little more black and white in his day, I think, and then too they hadn't discovered oil."

"What has oil got to do with it?" Jackie, involuntarily frowning, said on a suspicious, puzzled note.

"Merely that most of my cases have to do with that industry." He shrugged with mischievous unconcern. "Somehow I've gotten a reputation for being knowledgeable in the field."

Jackie just stopped herself from allowing a disgusted "Hmpf!" from betraying her discomfiture.

"Disappointed?" The quiet murmur confused her.

"What do you mean?" she said warily, unwilling to let him have his point if that was what he was requiring of her.

"Did you have me pictured as presiding over glamorous murder trials? Local celebrity divorces? Things of that nature?" he replied with a deepening smile that displayed the attractive crease to disgusting advantage.

With a shrug, Jackie turned her face away from him, afraid her desire to kiss the corner of his mouth might be displayed in her eyes. "I'm afraid I hadn't given your career all that much thought," she lied with haughty disdain, but her attempt at dismissal was betrayed by the slight surliness that had crept into her tone.

To her chagrin Adam laughed delightedly and reached over to take her hand in his own large, warm, unaccountably comforting one. Jackie tensed immediately and tried to pull away, but Adam's fingers tightened on hers, and the resulting electricity she felt was suddenly anything but comforting.

"Hadn't you?" he murmured with indulgent mockery in his tone, but to her relief he didn't pursue it. Instead he turned the conversation to focus on her.

"Well, *I've* wondered about yours," he said. "Tell me about yourself."

"Why?" Her suspicion of his genuine interest was evident.

"To make conversation?" he said with a droll note of humor. And then, becoming more serious, he added, "And because I'm interested."

He sounded sincere, and Jackie looked at him in pleased surprise. The hazel eyes stared back at her without the usual humor. Rather, they held a calm interested expectancy, and Jackie, feeling flattered in spite of herself, decided to accomplish the dual purpose of indulging his curiosity and taking her mind off her increasing physical awareness of him by acceding to his request.

Once she was launched into her biography, she found it was surprisingly easy to confide in Adam. He was a charming listener who laughed in all the right places, commented or questioned with just the right degree of interest, and drew her onward with such skill that Jackie found herself revealing much more and at much greater length than she had intended. The only real stumbling block in her discourse was when she reached the stage in her life where Matt had appeared.

She would have liked to skip that part entirely, feeling some slight degree of disloyalty in discussing her husband with the only other man in her life up to now who had shown any prospect of possibly becoming Matt's rival—at least in his ability to stir her senses. Yet Adam inquired directly, but gently. "How did you meet your husband?"

Hesitating, feeling slightly trapped by the question and unaware that her hand had clenched in Adam's, Jackie nevertheless answered. "At the newspaper where I went to work after going to San Francisco from Oklahoma."

As if sensing that Jackie needed to talk, regardless of her reluctance to do so, Adam took his time, but with quiet persistence drew her memories from her one by one. Finally, Jackie forgot about the trapped feeling and began to talk with unselfconscious naturalness about the happiness she had shared with Matt... and the deep depression she had slipped into upon his death, including her propensity for accidents, which sprang from her desire to join him. In the telling she became aware that she had advanced another step along the road to recovery. She didn't know why it should be so. She only knew it was.

Her voice died away at last. She glanced down at where their clasped hands lay between them on the couch, reflecting with mixed feelings of pleasure and anxiety that Adam's hand had begun to feel like an anchor of security, especially during her recounting of the years with Matt. She realized Adam must have been able to judge her emotional state very accurately while she had been talking, simply by virtue of whether she had tightened her grip or let her hand lie placidly in his, and she wondered if his insistence on maintaining the contact had sprung from a desire to give her emotional support or was simply a lawyer's trick to enable him to get to know what was behind the mask she, like all humans, wore.

Adam chose that moment to give her hand a slight

reassuring squeeze before letting it go, an action that made Jackie feel suddenly bereft. She pulled the released hand away as casually as she could and, clenching it with her other one, placed the pair of them in her lap. "I—I'm sorry." She faltered, embarrassed at having subjected Adam to such a detailed recounting of her personal affairs when they were virtually strangers. "I didn't mean to go on and on like that...."

Adam smiled faintly, his eyes reflecting a slight sadness. His tone was deep when he answered. "I'm flattered that you did. I have the feeling you haven't told anyone else these things—anyone other than your psychiatrist, that is." When Jackie didn't answer other than with a slight nod before twisting her head away to avoid his eyes, thinking he must be wondering what sort of a crazy person he had ended up with in the isolated cabin, Adam remarked, "Actually, I envy you."

Jackie jerked her head around to stare at him in wary amazement. Why should the great self-confident Adam Clarke envy *her*?

Adam's eyes were guilelessly sincere as Jackie searched them with her own. "You've had a happy marriage," he explained evenly. "That's more than a lot of people can say, including me. I've never even been married."

Deciding that a little judicial questioning was not out of order considering how freely she had spoken about her own life, she asked tentatively, "Have you ever considered it?"

A spark of delightful roguishness lightened his eyes,

making Jackie uncomfortably afraid he might have guessed her interest was more than casual. "Oh, yes," he answered lightly. "Once in college, again in my twenties, and"—he paused and flashed her a glance of barely suppressed amusement—"much more recently."

Jackie's heart sank, but then what had she expected anyway? she asked herself with morose resentment against the unknown recipient of Adam's affections. That a man as desirable as Adam could escape some woman's coils indefinitely? He must have been a target for most of his life, and even the wiliest of bachelors could eventually fall prey to the right woman if she came along at a weak moment, Jackie knew.

Adam was speaking again, and Jackie dragged herself back from her jealous peregrinations with difficulty to listen. "My college flame got impatient because I wanted to get my degree before settling down. She married someone else who was a great deal more impatient to make her his own," he drawled complacently. "I saw her recently and counted my blessings. It seems she had shrewish tendencies that escaped my notice in view of her more obvious, er, attributes."

Jackie thought with wrathful satisfaction that the lady's shrewish tendencies probably had their basis in regret at losing Adam.

He went on. "My second amour ended when I learned the woman of my choice had no intention of including children in our family unit. She felt there wouldn't be time for them in her busy schedule." His mouth quirked sardonically. "And she was right. She's on the staff of a very big law firm in Washington now, and I would have hated to have been responsible for clipping her wings."

Jackie thought his tone was entirely lacking in regret, which was encouraging, until she remembered that the lady lawyer was not his present love. No doubt whoever held his heart now was patient, motherly, sexy, beautiful, and entirely willing to submerge herself into Adam's life, she thought. Jackie hated the unknown paragon's guts wholeheartedly and hoped fervently that she would never have the displeasure of meeting her. She was praying she wouldn't have to sit and listen to Adam extoll the disgusting virtues of his intended when he took her by surprise.

"Why didn't you and Matt ever have children?" he asked with casual interest.

"We intended to," Jackie said after a moment of plunging back into the hurtful memories of the plans she and Matt had made. "In fact, we were trying when..." Her voice trailed off, and suddenly she was losing the ground she had gained so laboriously throughout the long months since Matt's death. To forestall that slippage she jumped to her feet and gathered the coffee cups, then walked with stiffened gait to the kitchen, where she deposited them on the counter next to the sink. She blinked her eyes rapidly to dispel the tears that were threatening to spill over and moved to the bedroom door. Adam had turned his body and was watching her, his chin resting on his fist. There was speculation in his eyes, a serious cast to his features, but he didn't apologize for triggering Jackie's reaction, and she was grateful he was leaving it alone.

"I'm sleepy," she said with abruptness. "I'm going to bed. Good night." She was halfway through the door when she heard his murmured reply.

"Sleep well, Jack. Don't let the bedbugs bite."

She winced at the combination of Matt's love name for her coupled with one of his favorite expressions at bedtime. Damn Adam Clarke! she thought. It was as though he had a script he was following to make her relive her happiness with Matt. Only he wasn't Matt— he was a stranger who was, in reality, completely different from her former husband. And there was no happy ending to look forward to at the end of this particular play. Adam was going to marry someone else, and she had better remember that the next time his nearness made her weaken into the old, familiar sexual response Matt had created, honed, and enjoyed to the full, she warned herself. Adam was not Matt.

Jackie went to the bed to turn down the covers and stopped short at seeing her lacy wisps of underwear spread over the quilt in tantalizing disarray. Adam *would* pick that particular drawer to unload for his own things, she fumed impotently. From the looks of it, he had enjoyed the process too, for the panties, bras, and filmy nightgowns were not placed in an orderly fashion as though he had lifted them out in one bundle. No, they gave the distinct impression of having been removed one by one, and Jackie felt her cheeks burning with a combination of privacy abused and disheartening excitement. How stupid could she get, she lashed herself unsparingly as she scooped up the garments and carried them to the bureau to cram them in among sweaters and slacks. Why should the thought of Adam's hands on these intimate personal belongings make her heart race and her stomach clench against the warm arousal that was invading her body? She *had* to get a hold on herself!

She remembered the long concealing flannel gown he had seen her in this morning and felt a perverse satisfaction in his knowing that it was not her usual sleepwear. She had worn it last night for warmth and comfort, knowing she was alone, but she had always loved the feminine sexy gowns that Matt had taken such pleasure in discarding. Adam knew she had them with her, and she hoped wrathfully that the thought of her wearing one would disturb his sleep as she was certain the thought of him on the other side of the door would rob her of hers.

For a moment she was even tempted to don one of them and saunter out through the living room on her way to use the bathroom. Still, that sort of flagrant provocation was beyond her, she knew, though she savored the contemplation of Adam's reaction with unholy satisfaction, embellishing the fantasy with imaginings of how she would disdainfully repel any advances he might make. But what if he didn't make any?

On that disheartening note she abandoned her fantasies for the mundane reality of preparing to sleep alone. She did, however, wear one of the prettier of her nightgowns, curling her lip in disgust at the flannel gown and stuffing it far to the rear of the drawer, out of sight. It was really too bad that Adam's first look at her had been while she was clad in that monstrosity, she reflected wistfully as she crawled between the sheets and flicked off the bedside lamp, for it was almost a certainty that she would never have the chance to erase that first impression and substitute one with far headier implications.

Chapter Six

The faint snick of a drawer opening brought Jackie out of a dream that was anything but pleasant. She seemed to have spent hours trying to crawl up a road that kept steepening until it was almost perpendicular, and along the way she had encountered various impediments, such as gaping potholes that threatened to swallow her up, vibrations that had almost tossed her over the sheer drops that bounded each side of the road, and a slippery surface that slid her back two steps for every one she took. She had reached the top the moment before awakening, only to feel the whole surface beneath her begin to tilt dangerously fast like a teeter-totter starting its descent.

"Ummmpf!" She woke with a start to find herself facing Adam's broad naked back where he sat on the edge of her bed, fumbling in one of the drawers of the bedside table. At her exclamation he turned his head to look down at her over his shoulder.

"Did I wake you?" he whispered politely. "Sorry. I need clean underwear." His explanation was delivered with a bare minimum of apology in his voice.

Jackie dragged the swatch of tousled hair that covered her face out of her eyes and glared at him. She was lying on her stomach with her face turned toward him, and the effort of looking up at the bland face that towered above her own increased her temper. With a groan she turned onto her back, unmindful that her action disclosed almost the whole of her bosom to his interested gaze.

"What time is it?" she gritted dangerously, covering her eyes with one hand to shut out the light shining through the open bedroom door from the living room.

"About five," he answered pleasantly. "It will be dawn soon."

This information provoked Jackie into an explosive, most unladylike oath. She was about to enlarge upon the observation when Adam interrupted her.

"Tsk, tsk," he scolded gently. "Not a morning person, are we?" He swiveled his hips around so that he was facing her, and the alarming tilt to the bed caused by his weight shifting made her realize where the teeter-totter effect of her dream had originated.

"*What* do you think you are doing?" She enunciated each word with scathing nastiness.

"I told you, I'm getting clean underwear," he replied with mild condemnation of her attitude clear in his patient, gentle voice.

"At *this* hour?" She took her hand away from her eyes and stared at him hatefully. "Are you out of your mind?"

Adam smiled at her and shook his head, but then his eyes traveled lingeringly over her face, down her neck, and on to where her breasts were heaving with outraged indignation. Jackie wanted to hit him and wipe off that disgustingly cheerful expression that indicated she was trapped into living with a man who *enjoyed* waking up before the sun. Even the birds had more sense than that.

"Why do you find it necessary to sit on my bed while you hunt for your crummy unmentionables?" she asked, the glint of desperate hostility in her eyes scorching him with its intensity.

Adam's smile grew broader, and Jackie could hardly believe the impression he gave of actually enjoying a confrontation with her at this ungodly hour. He ignored her question. "Do you know, I think while we're here I should make an effort to improve your disposition in the morning," he mused with thoughtful deliberation. "You seem to suffer from a bad case of the nasties in the early hours, and I hate to see someone miss out on the best time of the day, probably through a lack of proper training." He eyed her consideringly. "We'll start with teaching you how to say good morning in a pleasant voice."

"Drop dead!" was Jackie's snarling reply to his helpfulness.

"Jack..." Adam chided her warningly. "You're not even trying!" And he moved with lightning speed to pin her back onto her pillow as she made an effort to sit up, intending to push him off onto the floor, if that was possible, considering his size. He was barely suppressing his laughter as he held her struggling form with ease. "Now, let me hear you say it," he coaxed laughingly. "Say 'Good morning, Adam'"—

he paused to shift his body further onto hers to still her wild bucking movements—"and see if you can manage to smile at the same time, though if that's expecting too much of a first lesson, we can save it for the next!" His laughter and his pedantic tone enraged Jackie past the point of caution, not to mention his suppression of her movements.

"You overgrown bully, I'll see you in hell first!" she sputtered through her struggles, baring her teeth in a snarl of savage fury. "Who do you think you are, you monster—you pig—you—" She was searching for more descriptive adjectives when Adam calmly gathered up both of her hands in one of his huge ones, pinned them over her head, and used his other hand to shut her mouth, whereupon Jackie tried to bite him. He foiled her effort by squeezing her mouth into a pucker that was not painful, but exceedingly humiliating.

"Jack, Jack..." he said sadly, shaking his head with exaggerated regret. "I had hoped you would be amenable to my instruction without these unproductive histrionics. But since you're not..." He sighed heavily, but Jackie's eyes were riveted on the anticipatory gleam in his hazel ones, which belied his seeming disinclination for the coming disciplinary action. She was wondering half-hysterically what other diabolical humiliation he was about to inflict on her when he lowered his head and released her mouth in one smooth action before recapturing her lips with his own, and she found out just how far Adam Clarke would go with his unwelcome instruction.

Despite the immediate pleasure his mouth invoked

Jackie *had* to resist if only for the sake of her pride. She couldn't wrap her arms around his neck as she wanted to, because he still held her hands above her head, and she was exceedingly grateful that he did. After all, he couldn't know that the convulsive clenching of her fingers was more from a desire to run them through his hair than from a continued desire to strike him. And the trembling that seized her body could still be rage for all he knew, couldn't it? she wondered.

Jackie's pride was destined to desert her eventually, she found, for Adam was in no hurry to shorten his lesson. Little by little her struggles weakened, and she was never quite sure when she crossed over the line from supposedly unwilling student to boldly participatory equal to her teacher. Somewhere along the way she found that Adam had released her hands, and she was using them to caress his shoulders and stroke his hair. Farther down the path she realized that she was half out of her gown, and Adam's mouth had left her own to graze hungrily over her shoulders and then down to her breasts, where his tongue and teeth were busy provoking delightful sensations of pleasure that brought groans from her throat and encouragement from her lips instead of the invective she had spewed out earlier.

He ceased providing instruction in that direction all too soon, and lying full atop her, he began to kiss her again with slow deliberation, using his tongue as a sweet probe of discovery while Jackie lay back, savoring the feel of his muscular naked chest against her breasts. The bed linen was between them from the waist down, but it proved no barrier to the heat of arousal Jackie could feel in Adam's loins, or to the languorous response in her own.

Jackie was shivering delightedly, nonetheless, when Adam reached down to jerk the covers from between them, then settled back on top of her, his hands beneath her bottom and lifting her against that heat while he eased her thighs apart with his knee and took advantage of her vulnerable position to commence a slow circular movement with his hips that quickly changed her previous languor to hot excitement. There was only the barrier of his shorts and her silken gown between them, and grown suddenly greedy, Jackie was all for dispensing with those barriers, as well. She left it to Adam to pursue that objective in his own time, however, since his seduction so far had been entirely satisfactory.

He was in no hurry to take total possession, seemingly content for the moment to explore every silky inch of skin he could reach with his mouth and his hands. He slid down her body, trailing kisses and tasting flesh and leaving gooseflesh of pleasure wherever he touched. Jackie's fingers ran through his hair while she half-guided, half-submitted to his wayward travels.

When he reached the mound of flesh that was by now throbbing with the desire he had been intent upon creating and enhancing, she was disappointed when he merely planted one searching, drawing kiss and then started a return journey up her body that finished at her mouth, where he nibbled, nuzzled, and tasted to the full before taking her lips in a kiss that was a violent invasion and a graphic parallel of another act Jackie longed for with total concentration.

Her thoughts were a kaleidoscope of impressions, recording each new pleasure with a hungry anticipation for the next. She gasped with the need for breath when Adam finally released her mouth and raised his head to look at her, pressing his body forcefully against her hips and changing her gasp into a groan of need. "Good morning, Jack," he murmured huskily, brushing his mouth provokingly against hers, refusing to give in to her silent plea for more. He raised eyes darkened with passion to hers inquiringly, his smile sweet with prompting.

Jackie knew he wanted her capitulation and, recklessly, she gave it, smiling with equal sweetness at him, her eyes slumberous with desire. "Good morning, Adam," she whispered from deep in her throat, and was rewarded by the involuntary swallow and closing of his eyes that indicated his reaction to the seduction in her tone.

When she felt Adam move off her with an almost convulsive jerk that spelled out how difficult it was for him to make the effort, she should have been angry beyond measure, but she wasn't—not even when he said, "Now, see how pleasant early rising can be with a little effort?" His half-strangled, ragged tone brought a smile of commiseration to her lips, which she quickly suppressed as he turned to look at her. Poor Adam! she thought with tender amusement as she gravely nodded her concurrence to his words.

Poor Jackie! she thought a moment later when Adam cupped her face with one hand and stroked her mouth with his thumb. She wanted him back in the bed with her as badly as he obviously wanted to return, and was wondering why he was struggling so hard for restraint when it was obvious she was more than willing to continue the lesson.

"Do you know why I stopped?" he asked roughly, but the roughness was so evidently a result of formidable self-control of his arousal that Jackie couldn't take offense. She shook her head no, her eyes showing her bewilderment. "Because you probably haven't an ounce of protection, have you?" At Jackie's startled jerk and widened eyes he nodded ruefully. "I thought not."

Jackie felt her cheeks flaming with embarrassment. What did Adam think of her? What did her willingness tell him about how she felt about him, when she hadn't given a thought to such elementary precautions once embroiled in his lovemaking, she thought. She had gone off the pill shortly before Matt's death, as both of them had decided it was time to start a family. Afterward there had been no need to resume taking them—indeed, no *thought* of resuming their use.

"I didn't think...." She echoed her thoughts with self-defensive snappiness in her voice. *Oh, God, I'm such an idiot!*

"I know." Adam's tone was gentle. "I didn't give you a chance to think." He stood up and looked down at her, placing his hands on his hips and eyeing her thoughtfully. "It's probably just as well. You don't know me from"—he grinned suddenly, and the grin transformed his face into boyish glee at the pun he was about to make—"from Adam," he finished with a chuckle of satisfaction.

Jackie was not yet in a mood to enjoy his humor wholeheartedly, however. She was still struggling with her uncertainty over the unexpected ending to the passion that still warmed her veins. She smiled faintly and reached down to pull the sheet up over her exposed breasts. Adam noted her action with undisguised regret in his eyes, and his smile faded.

"Jack—" he started to say, but Jackie cut him off.

"Would you mind, Adam? I'm—I'm awake now. I'd like to get up and get dressed." She sounded like a silly little girl, she fumed inwardly, and making an effort, she smiled up at him. "I'll get breakfast while you bathe, shall I?"

Adam hesitated, seemed about to say more, then reconsidered. "All right." He nodded and reached into the still-open drawer to extract the clothing he had come for in the first place. He walked to the door and turned to give her a lopsided smile. "We'll start all over at breakfast, hmmm? We have some things to discuss."

Jackie felt a slight chill at his words, but she merely nodded, and as Adam left the room she stared at the closed door with a thoughtful sadness clouding her eyes. Of course they had things to discuss, she mused with a tinge of self-disgust. Like the woman Adam was contemplating marrying, for instance. No doubt Adam wanted to explain about her so that Jackie wouldn't get any ideas about furthering the relationship that had nearly become full-blown this morning.

She flung herself out of bed and began to search for

jeans and a sweater, keeping a tight rein on the hurt lurking just below the surface and waiting to attack. She mumbled to herself abstractedly as she dressed, excusing her own actions and Adam's. For her part she was lonely and had been denied closeness with anyone for months and months. No wonder all her subdued passion had broken through like a rocket in the face of Adam's appeal. Almost any woman would have found him impossible to resist, let alone someone like herself who had been without a man for so long.

And Adam? He was just an overgrown boy whose teasing had gotten out of hand. He was probably regretting it at this very moment, feeling guilty about almost betraying his intended with a woman he'd known barely forty-eight hours.

So how could she handle things so that the two of them could get through the next weeks without a repetition of this morning's fiasco? she wondered. Jackie faced her woebegone expression in the mirror and gave a helpless shrug. Quite honestly she didn't know, and unless Adam could come up with something, it might prove impossible to stay here, after all. She would just have to wait and see what he had to say at breakfast, she decided.

Jackie heard Adam bellowing in the bath as she came out of the bedroom and winced at his inability to carry a tune. Besides, what right had he to be so cheerful when her own spirits were wallowing in a pit of what seemed suspiciously like self-pity? she asked herself.

She scowled at the sight of his sleeping bag sprawled

untidily before the fireplace and disdained to roll it up. *Let him do his own housekeeping,* she thought with growing surliness, ignoring the fact that at least he had the fireplace roaring with a snapping fire.

The hiss of water as she was filling the coffee pot reminded her once again that she would have to wait until Adam finished with the bathroom before she could use it, and her frown became ferocious. "Damn, inconsiderate man!" she mumbled under her breath, forgetting that she herself had told him to go ahead and bathe.

By the time Adam sauntered out of the bathroom, Jackie was at the point of desperation, and she fairly flew by him to slam the door of the bathroom behind her with unnecessary force to the accompaniment of Adam's wicked grin. When she emerged a few moments later, her hair combed, but without having had time to wash up or brush her teeth, because she had left bacon frying on the stove, her temper had deteriorated to a boiling seethe.

Adam was folding up his sleeping bag and was whistling some obscene tune that exacerbated her raw nerves. She sailed by him with her nose in the air, and it was just as well he couldn't see the blue lightning flashing from her eyes. She managed to regain some control in the process of beating a bowl of pancake batter within an inch of its life, however, and by the time she had the table set and the first steaming platterful of pancakes in its place, she had settled down to feeling merely unfriendly without the desire to kill on sight.

Jackie stepped around the partition to call Adam to

breakfast and found him engaged in cleaning his hunting rifle. The sight reminded her that he was here to slaughter innocent deer, and her invitation to breakfast turned into a bark to "Come and get it!"

Adam looked up at her, startled at her tone, but she was already turning away to stomp back to the breakfast table and seat herself. When he joined her a few seconds later, she refused to look at him, but her face must have reflected her mood, because Adam sat silently for a moment, just looking at her, waiting until she put down her coffee cup before commenting.

His voice was quiet when he did speak. "I grew up with a custom I find hard to break," he said without censure, but there was a deep compelling sincerity in his voice that made Jackie raise her eyes to him warily. "My family always held hands." Then he reached over to grasp Jackie's in a warm light clasp that for all its seeming lack of force was as effectively binding as a steel chain. "And then we said grace," he added in that same deep tone that was impossible to protest. "Do you mind?"

Jackie could only shake her head no, having temporarily lost her voice in the confusion that raged in her mind. Adam was such a contradictory man, she thought with helplessness as he continued to hold her gaze, his eyes warm. He could be such a bully and then turn around and be the epitome of courteous, gentle manliness that had always been her ideal.

Adam didn't bow his head as he said the moving, comforting words of the short prayer. Indeed, as he delivered the grace in his beautifully modulated voice, deep and sure and compelling in its strength, he con-

tinued to hold her eyes with his own, and Jackie felt
the moisture of tears begin. But then he was done,
and with a final, brief squeeze of her hands, he released her and reached for his fork as calmly as
though the two of them had engaged in this ritual for
years.

Jackie was silent as she fumbled with trembling
fingers to pick up her own fork, thinking bewilderedly
that Adam Clarke had more facets to him than a dia-
mond, and that he was just as hard, and she suspected
just as purely fascinating as that particular gem.

Adam let her have her period of silence to recover
before he spoke again. "You disapprove of hunting,
don't you?" he asked with mild interest.

Jackie shifted lightly in her chair, discomfitted by
the return to normalcy after the moving experience of
a few moments before. Even though all signs of
temper had deserted her, she was compelled by honesty to answer him with the truth, yet she feared that
any prolonged discussion on the topic of hunting
would have them back at each other's throat in no
time.

"Yes," she answered him after a while, keeping her
reply brief in hopes that he would drop the subject.

"Do you know much about it?" he persisted.

Jackie hesitated, then decided to plunge. "I consider it a leftover primitiveness that allows men to
compensate for feelings of inadequacy by slaughtering
innocent animals," she said with determined mild-
ness. She only hoped she could continue to sound
mild. "It isn't necessary any longer to feed the family,
and I can't think of any justification for killing other

than that." She finished on a note of firm decisive-
ness.

Adam finished the bite of pancake in his mouth before replying, but his eyes were dancing with an emotion Jackie couldn't define. He took a sip of coffee
before continuing.

"Would you rather die by means of a quick bullet
or starve to death, Jackie?" The question was serious,
though the light continued to dance in his eyes.

Jackie frowned, looking at him as though trying to
discern the trap. She was certain there was one. "I'd
rather die by the bullet," she answered reluctantly,
feeling very much as though she were playing into his
hands. However, it was the truth, and she couldn't
answer differently.

"Ah," Adam replied, satisfaction in his tone.
"And would you deny that mercy to an animal?" he
persisted.

"No," Jackie said shortly, feeling more and more
backed into a corner.

"Neither would I," said Adam, his tone firm and
gentle. "And that's why I hunt." He held up his
hand, as Jackie would have protested. "Man has
killed off the predators that keep the numbers of deer
down where there's enough food for all of them," he
said in the tone of a teacher. One of the more successful teachers, Jackie had to admit, since there was no
hint of sneering superiority in his voice, only the reasonable tone of someone who was imparting information. "We killed off the predators because they, in
their turn, were killing the cattle that provide the
steaks you enjoyed so much last night."

Was there a hint of amusement behind his statement? she wondered. Jackie had to concede his point, though it went against the grain. Why should she object to hunting deer when she had never felt the slightest compunction about eating domestic animals who were slaughtered in the thousands to provide meat for people such as herself? she questioned. She felt a slight flush of reluctant embarrassment stain her cheeks, but Adam seemed not to notice as he went on.

"If hunters didn't keep the numbers down, the deer would reproduce to the point where many of them would starve to death, and in the process they denude their habitat where it's difficult for the ecology to recover." He smiled faintly with self-mockery. "Perhaps you still can't approve of it, but if I didn't feel there was that sort of justification for hunting, I wouldn't engage in it. I confess I enjoy the tramping about in this beautiful country more than the actual shooting, anyway. And if it helps any, I *do* eat the meat. I don't enjoy it as much as steak," he said with a wicked twinkle in his eye, "but when it's cooked right, it runs a close second."

Jackie was contemplating a way to concede his point of view—and, indeed, she found herself agreeing with him—without suffering too much from the sense of humiliating ignorance she was feeling, when Adam wound up his dissertation. "The government regulates the hunting, Jackie. Hunters are kept to strict limits, and most of them abide by the rules. They like the deer just as much as you do, though perhaps they're not as susceptible to their beautiful brown eyes as you are. Many of them are ranchers who have noted that cattle have beautiful eyes, as well."

His last statement succeeded in accomplishing her ignominious defeat, and Jackie dropped her eyes, from which her sense of shame could be easily detected, and reached for her cup of coffee in order to gain time before giving Adam his pound of flesh. He made it easier for her.

"Has my explanation succeeded in lifting the shroud of murderer from my persona?" he asked with deliberately humorous formality.

Jackie's lips twitched involuntarily, and then she was looking at Adam with a real smile on her lips and in her eyes, and she found it much less a hardship to give him his due, especially in view of the fact that Adam was watching her with an almost tender indulgence that brought a weakening to her knees and an increase in her pulse rate. "You are acquitted." She nodded her head with graceful formality. "The prisoner may leave the dock and resume his activities with exoneration from the court."

Adam laughed and gave an exaggerated sigh of relief. "Why, thankee, Judge," he drawled in an exaggerated western accent. He wiped his brow as though he'd been through a grueling experience. "I'll just mosey on back to the ranch, then, if that's all right with you?"

"Certainly," Jackie said haughtily. "Just as soon as you've paid your fine for presuming to teach the court a lesson." Her eyes were wicked with anticipation as she noted Adam's mock anxiety at the new development.

"A fine, ma'am?" he said meekly. "And what may that be? I warn you I'm a poor man and can't afford to pay much." His voice had taken on a whining quality Jackie was certain he'd heard from recalcitrants before the bench. And then he turned the tables on her by suddenly twirling an imaginary mustache and wiggling his eyebrows with wicked effect while his eyes leered at her suggestively. "But if the court could be persuaded to let me *work off* the fine?" His tone left no doubt as to what method of work he had in mind.

Jackie snorted with gleeful disgust. "That's *exactly* what I had in mind, sir," she said with sweet reasonableness. "And you can start by doing the breakfast dishes," she added with a hoot of laughter as his leering anticipation turned to dismayed injury.

He shook his head and sighed pitifully. "It's a cruel world, and that's a fact," he said sadly. "There ain't no justice anywhere."

"You'd know more about that than me," Jackie retorted with dry humor. "And if you have a guilty conscience, well..." She rose to her feet and gave him a saucy look. "Don't they always say the devil finds work for idle hands? Get busy, and before you know it, you'll feel *so* much better." She cooed the last words at him and sashayed to her bedroom to gather clean clothing, intending to take her bath at her leisure while Adam did the cleaning up in the kitchen.

Adam stopped her before she reached the door. "Jack..." She felt a small shiver of gladness that he was back to calling her that instead of Jackie. She had found she hadn't liked hearing it on his lips when she associated the shorter name with more intimate moments between them.

She turned back to face him. "Yes?" she said inquiringly.

"Don't we have some talking to do on a subject other than hunting?" he asked softly.

Jackie felt a return of the dread she had felt when he had said earlier that they would talk over what had happened between them this morning, but she forced herself to return to the table and seat herself, nervously pouring another cup of coffee to have something to do with her hands.

Adam watched her in silence for a moment, and it was all Jackie could do to stop herself from fidgeting. Finally, completely out of the blue, he remarked, "I have a sister about your age." Jackie shot a bewildered look at him as he continued with bland unconcern. "She's nothing like you, except that... well, she's inclined to let her heart rule her instead of her head, as I think you do."

Jackie stopped herself from uttering an instinctive denial, knowing that there was some truth in Adam's assessment of her character, and feeling increasingly uneasy as she wondered if Adam was about to tell her that what had happened between them this morning was a momentary aberration they should both forget.

"Her first marriage was happy, though childless— pretty much a parallel to yours," Adam went on quietly. "Her husband was killed, and she went through hell for a while before she met a man who was extremely attractive to her—sexually."

Jackie stiffened, sensing all at once where Adam

was going with his seemingly irrelevant conversation, and aware, for reasons she couldn't decipher just yet, that she didn't want to go along with him. But Adam was unstoppable once he got started, and since Jackie had no valid excuse for objecting, she was forced to listen silently.

Adam's tone was dry and a muscle twitched in his jaw as he continued. "This man seduced my sister before she was fully over her husband's death. She needed to love again, but she jumped in before she was ready for another relationship. Unfortunately, she got pregnant, and the man insisted they get married because of it—as almost any decent man would who had sired a child."

Jackie's cheeks burned with embarrassment at Adam's words. The parallels were clear, of course. If it had been up to her to exercise control that morning, she might very well have ended up pregnant herself. It had been up to Adam to behave like a responsible adult, and he had, but somehow she didn't feel the gratitude she should have toward him, perhaps because it was painful to realize she had behaved so foolishly. How galling to have been so stupid, she thought. She wondered wryly if Dr. Chelski would be proud of her for taking his advice or ashamed of her for taking it so wholeheartedly.

"The marriage didn't work out." Adam interrupted her thoughts in a clipped voice. "He was a city person, and she was a Montana country girl. He wanted a sophisticated helpmate to assist him up the ladder of success; she wanted a quiet life with her husband and her child. But mostly it didn't work out because"—Adam fixed her with a grim look that made Jackie freeze with apprehension—"he couldn't compete with her first husband."

Jackie's eyes widened as she took in the implications of Adam's words and related them to what Dr. Chelski had said to her: that she wouldn't let Matt go; that no man could compete with a ghost. As her eyes locked with Adam's she wondered if Dr. Chelski's—and apparently Adam's—assessment of what she was doing still held true. She didn't know, she realized.

"As a result," Adam went on, still in that grim tone, "my sister is afraid to ever try again. She centers her whole life on the child, who, incidentally, almost never sees his father. It's not a very satisfactory situation any way you look at it." He leaned back in his chair, took a deep breath, and eyed her intently. "And it all could have been avoided if she had grieved properly, then let her husband die once and for all, instead of rushing into an incompatible relationship before she was prepared to take the consequences, simply out of a need for ... touching, shall we say?"

Jackie was feeling angrily confused and more than a little put down, and she reacted instinctively. She drew back in her chair, folded her arms belligerently over her breasts, and faced Adam with fire in her eyes. "And what would the wise Adam Clarke suggest for someone like ... his sister?" She paused meaningfully before the last two words, and when they came out, her tone was sarcastic.

Adam's look was closed and cautious, but his eyes

were unflinching. "He would suggest taking the time to get to know someone before falling into bed with them," he said quietly, "and, above all, that she get over one man before taking up with another."

All pretense that they were talking about Adam's sister flew out the window in the face of Jackie's outrage at what she considered Adam's self-righteous condemnation of her. "I didn't fall in bed with you," she stormed at him, abandoning her self-protective posture to pound her fists angrily on the table. "You fell in bed with me!"

"So I did," Adam responded calmly, but with a glint in his eyes that said he wasn't going to back away from this battle. "Right into your open arms."

"They weren't open until you forced them to be!"

"Touché! But a man would have had to be a saint to resist such a temptation."

"I didn't tempt," Jackie wailed in frustration, wanting to reach across the table and choke an admission of her innocence from Adam.

"Not purposefully," Adam admitted grimly, affording her some gratification. "But from the moment you reached puberty, you were a born temptress. Didn't your precious Matt ever tell you what happens to a man when you so much as look at him out of those big blue eyes? Not to mention when you cuddle up to him with that warm woman's body and kiss him as though you want to eat him alive?"

Jackie had had enough. Where did Adam Clarke get off chastising her for being attractive, for God's sake? And why was it suddenly all her fault that the great Adam Clarke had been tempted when it had been *he* who had pounced on *her* like a hungry fox on a tender rabbit in the bed this morning! she wanted to know.

After jumping to her feet, Jackie placed her hands on her hips. "I knew this wouldn't work," she ground out angrily. "But, no, the wonderful, wise, all-knowing Adam Clarke insisted that it could! That he would keep his distance, and we would live together like two old hunting buddies! Ha!" she snarled, then blew a wisp of hair out of her right eye, looking for all the world like a fighter facing off an opponent, which she was.

"Now, you listen to me," she pronounced warningly. "I didn't ask for this arrangement, and I certainly didn't ask you to crawl in my bed this morning. For God's sake, why do you think I came out to this isolated cabin in the first place?" she stormed scathingly. "To find men like you to *entice* with my nasty womanly wiles?" She bent toward Adam, who sat calmly facing her attack and with a disgusting humorous light in his eye that just made Jackie all the madder.

"Well, I didn't!" Jackie answered her own question with outrage in her tone. "Not only didn't I come here to tempt anybody, but I contradicted my doctor's direct order to do just that!" She felt triumphant when she saw Adam's surprise. "Oh, yes." She followed up her advantage quickly. "I'm under strict orders to fall all over the first man who's even one-*third* as acceptable—and that's a direct quote from my doctor—as Matt was to me. Just wait until I tell him where following his advice got me! I'm sure he never expected it to lead to my being castigated for being a wanton, humiliated for being human and denigrated for responding to direct provocation!''

To her utter amazement Adam's reaction to her stormy accusations was a lazy smile. "And am I?" he asked disconcertingly.

"Are you what?" Jackie yelled at him.

"One-third as acceptable to you as Matt was?" he asked calmly.

Jackie reached both hands to her hair in a gesture indicative of her utter frustration. "Yes, yes, yes! Why else would I have lost my head like that this morning?"

"Is that all?" Adam persisted.

Jackie lowered her hands and glowered at him wearily, her anger dissipating into complete bewilderment at his failure to react as she expected—at any time, on any matter. "Is that all what?" she asked with despair.

"Am I only one-*third* as acceptable?" he responded with patience, as though talking to a child.

Jackie stared at him in confusion. "I don't know," she said in a weak voice. "I don't know anything right now." Then she added abstractedly, "Except that I don't think you're quite human."

"Oh, I'm human, all right," Adam said with a slight return to grimness. And then as Jackie just looked at him with all the weary confusion she was feeling, he got to his feet and came to her, placing one arm around her waist and tipping her head up to look into her eyes. "Jackie, I'm sorry if you thought I was accusing you of anything. I wasn't." And at her skeptical look he amended. "Well, maybe you did pierce my armor more than I'm accustomed to. When I came here, I never expected to share the cabin with a woman who can test my willpower to the limits." He grinned with charming insouciance and a grating lack of repentence at her, and Jackie began to glare frostily again.

"I don't quite know how it happened, but somehow we got off the subject." Adam acted quickly to forestall another storm. "I didn't intend to make you angry. I just thought, in view of the...er...volatile situation we have here, that we should get some things out in the open before things go any further."

"Such as what?" Jackie asked with suspicious belligerence, twisting her chin out of Adam's grip and eyeing him warily.

Adam gave a slight smile, and his eyes were steady as he looked into Jackie's. "Such as whether we're going to take the necessary steps to make an affair possible," he enumerated, ignoring Jackie's widened eyes and somewhat panicky look. "Or whether we're going to go the platonic route—if that's possible now," he added dryly, "until we get to know one another better. Or whether one of us is going to clear out of here before this electricity between us gets out of hand and one of us gets hurt."

Jackie stalled. "Who—ah—do you think might get hurt?" she asked hesitantly.

"Me." Adam's straightforward admission melted some of Jackie's anger and made her curious.

"Why do you think you might get hurt?" she asked in a puzzled tone.

Adam's expression was soberly grim, adding a maturity to his face that made Jackie feel a little out of her depth in relation to him. His hazel eyes roamed her face dispassionately while he spoke, but his words were anything but dispassionate. "I'm thirty-seven years old, Jackie. I've been close to being in love before, but never to the extent that I've lost my head. Where you're concerned, however, I have the distinct feeling I may not only lose my head, but my heart, as well. It's a damn uncomfortable proposition to face at my age."

An involuntary smile curved Jackie's sweetly sensuous mouth as she warmed to Adam's admission that he found her a danger to his self-control, but Adam didn't smile back. He was deadly serious, and Jackie's smile faltered as he went on. "I don't play second fiddle to anyone, Jackie—especially not to a dead man I can't compete with on a rational basis." Jackie's expression sobered to match Adam's. "I'm not sure you're ready yet to give up Matt's memory for a live man's love. I'm not even sure we have anything going for us other than an explosive sexual attraction. And until I *am* sure, I'm reluctant—not unwilling," Adam added with a wry sensuous smile, "but *reluctant*—to rush into a headlong affair with you. Not that I'm sure we can continue to live here together without having one."

Jackie blinked up at him, besieged by the dilemma he had outlined so clearly. She couldn't reassure him that she was ready to love again, because she didn't know if that was true. All she knew was that she melted in Adam's arms, that she was jealous of the woman he had said he was considering marrying, and that she genuinely *liked* Adam despite his contradictory refusal to behave predictably. She got sidetracked—perhaps purposefully—by the remembrance of that woman.

"Adam, are you considering marrying a woman back in Montana?" she asked, irrational jealousy tinging her voice.

"Damn it, Jackie, will you stick to the point?" he responded exasperatedly.

"Surely the question of whether you're already committed to someone else *is* a valid point in this discussion?" she asked with some spirit.

"There is someone, but I'm not committed," he said shortly. "Now, are you through circling the real issue?"

"No, I'm not," she shot back, her temper rising again. "That woman is an issue. I want to know about her."

"You don't have any right to know about her—not yet, anyway," Adam said with brutal frankness, causing Jackie's chin to tauten stubbornly. Then, with a sigh of tolerant resignation, Adam relented. "I'm ready to get married, Jackie. The woman in Montana is—suitable. I've given it some thought. I was even pretty well determined to ask her . . . until I met you." The last was said with a certain amount of grim exasperation that made Jackie want to flare up at him again and tell him that if he found the attraction he felt for her so intolerable, then his idea that one of them should leave here was a good one. She didn't say a word, however; she suddenly found the idea of their separating before they'd had a chance to explore the possibilities of a relationship between them entirely unacceptable.

Jackie started to draw away from Adam's hold, needing some space and time in which to explore her feelings about such a possibility, but Adam held her where she was and pinned her with one of his intent stares. "What do you want to do, Jackie?" he asked with a note of determination to receive an answer in his voice. "Do you want to have an affair?"

Jackie winced, her sensibilities somewhat offended by Adam's bluntness. "Yes and no," she forced herself to answer in a small voice.

"What the hell does that mean?" he asked, his voice rising on a note of anger that showed he had a temper every bit as volatile as hers.

"Just what I said," she answered stubbornly. "I know you can make me want you—you proved that this morning. But I don't know if it's a good idea for all the reasons you brought up a few minutes ago."

"Do you want one of us to leave, then?" he asked on an ominous note.

"No." Again the small voice.

"Then you want to keep it platonic until we know one another better?" He persisted in pinning her to the wall.

"I don't know!" Jackie wailed, feeling trapped by his persistence. "It's hard to have a platonic relationship when you want—you want—"

"*Who* wants?" he insisted on a hard note.

"I want...you want...we both *want*..." Jackie felt pressed beyond endurance by his insistence on wring-

ing every little concession from her. Didn't he have
any tact at all? she asked herself.

"You're damn right we both want," Adam said on
a savage growl as he pulled her up hard against his
body. "And how the hell do you think we're going to
sleep in the same cabin when every time we look at
each other we want this"—he brought his head down
and opened his mouth over hers in a devastating demonstration of dominant hunger—"and this..." he
muttered against her mouth as he brought a hand up
to her breast, capturing its fullness in his palm and
stroking the nipple with a relentless thumb, "and
this..." he groaned as he slipped a hand under her
bottom to press her against his throbbing warmth.

Jackie quite unashamedly reveled in his need, and
in the need he was creating in her. She forgot all the
unanswered questions they both had as she bent to his
will and melted into him, delighting in his hard male
strength against her softness. She felt at home, at
peace—a riotously passionate peace, true, but peace
all the same—as though she belonged again, as
though she had found her other half again. She
moaned his name, "Adam...Adam..." over and
over again as she stroked the masculine shoulders that
were so taut with the desire to crush her into him but
the self-control he exercised not to hurt her.

And then he was pushing her away, staring down at
her with a glazed desperate need in his eyes, tinged
with an almost bitter question. "At least you know my
name," he said on an indrawn breath. "But do you
know it's me holding you like this...making love to
you like this? Or are you fantasizing that I'm Matt?"

"Adam!" Jackie's shocked incredulity was evident in her voice and in the pained look in her eyes.

Adam's jaw tightened and his hands hurt where he gripped her shoulders, and then with effort he relaxed. "I'm sorry," he grated out. "But I can't keep from asking myself that question. I've got to know."

"Oh, Adam." Jackie shook her head, her confusion and apprehension evident in her face.

Adam stepped back and let her go. "I've got to think, Jackie," he said, rubbing his hand over his hair in frustration. "This is the first time in my life I can remember not knowing how to handle a situation." He walked over to grab a jacket and started toward the door. "I'm going out for a walk. Maybe when I come back we can decide what to do. Right now I'm too worked up to think straight."

Jackie watched him go, feeling as frustrated as he looked. When the door closed behind him, she slumped down into a chair, wondering how things had come to this point in two short days. And she had thought she was coming to Wyoming to bask in isolation and work on a novel! Instead she was being invaded by enough contradictory emotions to fill one while Adam's presence was as far from isolation as she could possibly get, she realized.

Chapter Seven

By the time Jackie had bathed and straightened the cabin, Adam was back from his walk, but it didn't seem to have improved his mood. Indeed, he seemed so preoccupied that Jackie had to ask him three times if he wanted a substantial meal for lunch or merely sandwiches. Finally, he muttered something about doing a little reconnoitering of the area before hunting season officially started the next day and that he would take sandwiches with him. When he had them ready, he left again, and in her present confused mood, Jackie was not sorry to see him go.

She was almost tempted to pack her bags, turn tail, and run. Almost, but not quite. The thing to do, she instructed herself as she put together a beef stew to simmer on the stove for dinner, was to get some perspective on the matter—enumerate the facts, assimilate the data, and come up with a plan of action.

Once the stew was prepared she pulled on a jacket and set out for a "thinking" walk of her own, heading for the clearing she had found the day before, where the atmosphere was so conducive to peaceful thought.

Once there, she was content to sit for a few moments and take in the glorious fall foliage that turned the surrounding forest into a wonderland of color. Orange and yellow and red leaves formed patterns of incredible beauty, and Jackie bestirred herself to gather a vaseful of branches with leaves attached, picturing how pleasant the arrangement would look on the kitchen table.

The sun was warm, the air was exhilarating, the stream babbled, the squirrels chittered, and Jackie took it all in with every sense expanding to encompass her surroundings, until at last she felt calm enough to begin thinking about Adam Clarke and the dilemmas his intrusion into her life presented.

What were the facts? she asked herself doggedly. One, she had known Adam two short days. And even though she had fallen in love with Matt in an equivalent amount of time, it didn't follow that she had to repeat the process with Adam. True, she was trembling on the brink, but there was still time to pull back, she knew.

Two, it was apparent that Adam had some real doubts about starting up a relationship with her, even though it was equally apparent he was tremendously attracted to her—physically. Perhaps that was why Adam had his doubts, Jackie mused. Adam didn't seem to like being so strongly attracted to a woman— he wasn't in full control of the situation. Perhaps as a judge he had gotten so used to being the arbitrator of other people's fates—and having been single so long, the arbitrator of his own—that he was intensely opposed to putting himself into another's power.

Jackie absently threw pebbles into the brook as she contemplated that she didn't much favor becoming vulnerable to a man's power over her again, either. It hurt so much when the love disappeared, and she didn't know if she could stand going through another such loss if she gave her heart to Adam and then something happened to him as it had to Matt.

Still, she thought, a soft smile of remembrance curving her lips, in Matt's case the years they had had together had been worth the agony of losing him. But would the same hold true with Adam? she wondered. Her smile turned into a frown as she remembered his worries that she wasn't over Matt—that she only wanted a man's body next to hers in a warm bed to make her forget for a time that she didn't have Matt any longer.

Was that true? she asked herself, sighing heavily. Did she really want a real replacement for Matt, or simply a temporary substitute to warm her bed at night? And if that was all she wanted, was it fair to Adam to use him that way, knowing he might fall so deeply in love with her that he could be seriously hurt if she found herself unable to make a lasting commitment to him? On the other side of the coin, however, was it fair to deny herself the opportunity to love again on the off chance that Adam, a grown man, might get hurt in the process if things didn't work out? she wondered.

Jackie scowled at an innocent squirrel who had ventured into the clearing, not really seeing the creature, she was so immersed in her thoughts. The squirrel, however, not being privy to the fact that he was not the object of her hostility, took one look and turned tail to depart into the safer environs of the surrounding trees.

What was she to do? The question revolved in her head like a recurring nightmare, exacerbating her nerves until Jackie wished she'd never set eyes on Adam Clarke. Life had been so peaceful without him...so peaceful and so dull.

Jumping to her feet, she struck out at a brisk pace, in keeping with her churning thoughts, following the brook and a faint roaring sound that drew her onward like a magnet. Gradually the brook widened into a small pool, which culminated in a waterfall that tumbled off the edge of a cliff in joyful exuberance to join a full-scale river at the bottom.

Entranced by the sight, Jackie stood on the edge and peered down at the wild beauty, determining that sometime in the near future she would descend that cliff and explore the area at its base. Perhaps she would bring a picnic lunch and spend the whole day, taking a minivacation from writing her novel. The thought of the novel brought with it a sense of guilt that she hadn't yet made a start on it, however, and reluctantly she turned her steps back to the cabin.

As she retraced her steps Jackie decided that contrary to her usual need to take charge of a situation, she would let Adam handle this one. Since she couldn't come to a decision, anyway, she would let *him* decide where he wanted their relationship to go. If he wanted an affair, she knew she couldn't resist him. If he wanted a platonic relationship, which she privately considered the most sensible course of action until they knew one another better—but she knew also that common sense flew out the window when they touched one another—then she would refrain from tempting him. And if he wanted to leave here, she wouldn't attempt to stop him, though she knew that was the one solution to their problem she least favored.

With a certain degree of serenity at having given the initiative to Adam, Jackie entered the cabin and faced her typewriter with a renewed sense of energy. And it was with almost no sense of surprise that she found herself tapping out the character sketches and outline of a love story rather than the historical novel about Oklahoma's early days that she had planned to write. But when she later read over the pages she had typed, she *was* surprised to find that her hero bore a striking resemblance to one Adam Clarke rather than Matt Roth.

Jackie was still contemplating that surprising fact when Adam returned as she was stirring up a batch of biscuits to go with the stew. Her heart gave an involuntary surge of gladness that he was back, though her greeting was matter-of-fact.

"Hi. Did you have a good day?"

Adam's eyes took all of her in, in a single sweeping glance that left her feeling naked before his gaze, and he replied with a small smile tugging at his mouth that seemed peculiarly self-mocking. "It was a most rewarding day," he answered casually. "I located some good hunting areas. I even spotted a doe once, but needless to say she was reluctant to strike up an acquaintance." He laughed softly, and Jackie thought she detected a certain sly purpose behind his next words. "I intend to convince her she has nothing to fear from me if she'll ever again let me get close enough to sweet-talk her. Only the bucks are fair game, you know."

Jackie smiled briefly, relieved that his mood was so good but rather puzzled by his tone. "Is that so?" she said, striving to maintain an attitude of pleasant, cooperative interest. "Poor darlings. It isn't easy to be a male, is it?"

"You don't know the half of it," Adam murmured with a gleam of dry humor in his eyes. Then he changed the subject. "Would you like a drink? I was going to fix myself one to chase the dust out of my throat."

"That sounds wonderful," Jackie said enthusiastically. "We'll just have time before the biscuits are done. I've made a stew. I hope you like it."

"Love it," Adam declared. "White wine suit you?"

"Fine." Jackie watched with adoring eyes as Adam crossed the room to get the bottle out of the refrigerator, then quickly resumed an expression of pleasant companionableness as he faced her again, in keeping with her determination not to tempt him.

"Will I have time to wash up?" Adam inquired after pouring the wine. "I traveled some rough country today."

"Of course." Jackie was moving toward the table to set it for supper. "I'll finish in here while you're doing that."

"Hmmm..." Adam was leaning back against the counter, unknowingly presenting his physique to advantage, but becoming aware of it rapidly as Jackie's eyes roamed his skin-tight jeans and masculine shoulders. "If we could delay dinner for a while, I could have a bath, and you could wash my back," he murmured in a soft seductive voice.

Jackie swallowed, her expressive features showing clearly that the idea was not without appeal. Still, she was not yet ready to plunge so drastically into *that* intimate an endeavor. She attempted a weak joke to cover her confusion. "Sorry, but the biscuits won't stand for any delay. They're not one of my fortes, but if we eat them warm, they're at least swallowable. Once they're cold they're members of the rock family."

Adam shrugged unconcernedly, but his eyes sparkled with knowing challenge, indicating he was perfectly aware that Jackie was letting cowardice win over her real inclination. "My loss," he said with a regretful grin.

No, mine! Jackie corrected him silently, her eyes lingering on his body with longing. Then she gave herself a mental shake and turned her back on Adam's appeal.

While Adam was in the bathroom Jackie set the table speedily, then stood back and debated whether it would be just a bit too much if she added candles to complete the attractive arrangement of fall leaves that held pride of place in the center of the table. No, candles would be entirely too blatant an invitation, so she discarded the idea regretfully. They would have the fireplace after dinner, which was even more effective for staging a romantic scene if one should happen to develop. Not that she expected one, she scolded herself hastily. She was getting carried away with her fantasies, and there was no point to that until Adam made it plain how he wanted things to be between them.

When Adam joined her at the table, the scent of his after-shave mingled with the delicious aroma of stew and hot biscuits, and Jackie shot a quick surreptitious look at him, noting that his face looked suspiciously smooth for a man who had a heavy beard growth and had shaved so many hours ago. She felt a little zing of pleasure that he had made the effort. Of course, he could be just the type of man who felt it obligatory to shave before dinner, but since it was much more satisfactory to believe he had done it solely for her benefit, she decided to do just that.

As the meal progressed it seemed to Jackie that they could have been seated in the most elegant restaurant San Francisco boasted, eating gourmet fare, if one judged by their manners. To her pleasure she learned that Adam possessed a most sophisticated line of banter that sparked off her own not inconsiderable wit. She found herself wishing after a while that she *had* used the candles, for they would have put the finishing touch on her ability to imagine herself being courted in a style dear to almost any woman's heart.

Once or twice she remembered to caution herself that Adam might *not* be courting her, but merely exerting his charm to make their time together more enjoyable. But it was so much more tempting to believe otherwise, that at last she abandoned good sense altogether and began to flirt with unselfconscious naturalness, positively reveling in the fact that Adam was giving every indication he was vulnerable to her wiles. If, indeed, they were wiles, for she was not conscious of acting in any way other than entirely naturally. If her eyes softened when Adam's gaze held hers, she was not aware of it. If her mouth pouted enticingly at one of his more outrageous jokes, it was not done with the purpose of making him want to kiss her. If her voice grew more seductively husky each time she spoke, why, it was due to the wine, not to any conscious plan to seduce him.

"Tell me about Montana," she invited with a dreamy look in her eyes. "I've heard it's beautiful."

"It is," Adam said with sincerity. "Though it's not as sophisticated or exciting as San Francisco."

Was he testing her? Jackie wondered. Did he wonder if she would be willing to give up the allure of San Francisco for the countryside of Montana? She smiled a secret inner smile, determined to put his fears to rest. "I grew up in a small town in Oklahoma," she reminded him calmly. "And though I like San Francisco, I love the country, too." And having planted that thought in his mind—though why she felt compelled to do so was unclear to her—she again invited him to tell her about his home.

"It's big but uncrowded. The sky is bluer than anywhere else I've ever seen. It's clean and natural and it makes my soul feel good to be there," he said simply. "You'll have to see it to really appreciate it, though. Words are inadequate."

"And you never want to live anyplace else," Jackie stated with certainty, her eyes fondly roaming his rugged face.

"No." The word was firm, and Adam's eyes pierced her with intensity as he asked almost casually. "Does it sound like a place you'd like?"

Jackie smiled sweetly at him. "Yes, Adam. It sounds like a place I'd like. Do you have me pictured as the ultimate city girl?"

He hesitated, then said softly, "I thought you might be. I confess I'd forgotten you grew up in a small town." He shrugged then. "Of course, I live in Missoula, which is a fairly large city, though it can't compare with San Francisco."

A smidgeon irritated with Adam's harping on the appeal of San Francisco, Jackie said firmly, "San Francisco is a nice place to live, Adam, but it may be an even nicer place to visit occasionally. Now, have we settled the fact that I'm not tied with iron strings to the place?"

Adam looked momentarily startled, then his face creased into a wide grin. "Was I that obvious?" he asked.

"You were." She nodded, then deciding to have a little of her own back, she said with a touch of wryness, "I wonder, Adam, if Montana is so appealing, why you decided to come to Wyoming for your vacation instead of staying there?"

He grinned again. "Habit. My family used to live here, and I got used to coming here." Then his grin faded somewhat. "And this time I wanted familiar surroundings in which to do some serious thinking."

Inwardly Jackie stiffened, but her face showed nothing of the trepidation she was feeling. "About

asking a certain woman in Montana to marry you?"
she asked calmly.

Adam's expression grew serious. "Yes." He hesitated, then apparently decided to be as honest and confiding about himself as Jackie had been on the previous night. "As I told you this morning, I'm thirty-seven and I've been thinking for some time that if I want children and a family, it's time to get on with it. The only drawback has been that I've never found anyone I loved enough to marry."

"You aren't in love with this woman?" Jackie asked cautiously, unsure if she had the right to ask such a personal question.

"I'm not sure how to answer that," Adam replied with disappointing honesty. "I like her. I admire her. I know she'd make a good mother and a good wife..
and a good lover."

Jackie felt her cheeks growing warm, whether with temper or embarrassment she wasn't sure. "Then what's the problem?" she asked somewhat stiffly.

Adam reached over to cover Jackie's hand with his own, a gesture that dispelled, but only somewhat, the jealousy she was feeling. "The problem is," he said softly, "that I've met a fiery, hot-tempered, hot-blooded witch who makes what I feel for the woman in Montana seem tame and inadequate. I only wish I knew which emotion makes the best foundation for a marriage—passion or warm friendship."

Feeling somewhat affronted, Jackie spoke spiritedly. "What makes you think the two are mutually exclusive? Matt and I had both!"

Jackie could have bitten her tongue out when she

saw Adam's expression close up. Why, she wondered, furious with herself, did she have to bring up Matt's name right now? And equally furiously, she wondered why she should have to censor Matt's name from her vocabulary simply because Adam was convinced she would never get over her former husband? Matt had been a part of her life for seven years. How was she supposed to pretend he hadn't existed? she asked herself.

She watched with resentful anxiety as Adam fought down some strong emotion he was laboring under, and when he had it under control, he remarked with only a trace of sarcasm, "Yes, I'd forgotten. You and Matt had the perfect marriage, didn't you?"

Her temper was flaring again, and Jackie nodded defiantly. "Absolutely perfect," she agreed heatedly. Some imp of devilment made her add "And, of course, there's not a man on earth who can compete with Matt. There aren't any good enough!"

Later she reflected that she must already, unknowingly, have judged Adam's character with amazing accuracy. A competitive man, he would never settle for being bested, much less by a dead man. But then she watched with growing fearfulness as the anger rose in Adam's eyes, his jaw firmed, his muscles tensed, and he got ready to do battle with his rival.

"Is that so?" he asked in a menacing murmur as he got slowly to his feet and circled the table toward her. Jackie started to get up and flee what she had provoked, but Adam's hand shot down to close over her wrist and pull her to her feet. "But that's not entirely true, is it?" he asked rhetorically as he clamped her reluctant body to his own. "There's one area where I doubt if even the great Matt Roth could evoke a better response than I can, isn't there, Jack?"

"Adam..." Jackie started to plead as she stared into his eyes, seeing the invincible purpose there and feeling almost afraid of him. "I'm sorry...I didn't mean to—"

But she got no further as Adam's mouth captured hers in a brutal kiss that quickly changed to persuasive seductiveness when Jackie's moan made it evident that he was hurting her and therefore defeating his purpose. A few seconds later Jackie had to admit, with slumberous passion, that Adam was entirely right. In that area, at least, he was Matt's equal in every way.

If Jackie had been capable of coherent thought, she would have recognized that Adam was bent on reducing her to mindless pleading for his possession out of his own need to replace Matt's memory in her mind and heart and body with his own living presence, but thought proved impossible as Adam's assault on her senses grew in intensity and effectiveness by the second.

His mouth plundered hers with soft dominance, wet and hot and deliciously invasive. Yet when he had her totally centered on the erotic interplay of their tongues and teeth and lips, he shifted direction, sliding his mouth delicately over her cheek to the hollow behind her ear, where he nibbled and probed with his tongue until she was leaning into his body for support against the weightlessness her instinctive desire created.

Adam's hands were not idle, either. They worked

in concert with his mouth, molding her pliant softness
against his hard muscles, traveling from her shoulders
to her hips, kneading and massaging her flesh into
tingling awareness of the warm magic of his fingers
and palms. She began purring like a kitten between
moans and gasps of pleasure under his manipulations.

It seemed entirely natural when he lifted her into
his arms to carry her to the couch in front of the fireplace, and when he laid her gently down, Jackie's
arms pulled him with her until they were settled body
against body among the soft cushions.

Now Jackie could indulge her own wish to touch
him as he was touching her, to explore the smooth
warmth of his flesh beneath his shirt, the hard contours of his muscles beneath that flesh. In mutual
agreement each undid the impeding buttons of the
other's clothing until their upper bodies were bare to
hungry eyes and hungry hands and searching lips.

"You are so beautiful, so smooth, so warm...so
giving..." Adam muttered in a half-strangled voice
that echoed his arousal, which Jackie could feel
against her trembling thighs.

Jackie gasped as he ended his accolade by closing
his tender, seeking mouth over the ripe tautness of
her nipple to draw rippling sensations of mindless
pleasure from her.

"Ah, Adam..." she groaned, ceasing her provocative hip motions temporarily to draw him closer to her
in an effort to feel all of him at once. "You make me
feel beautiful and warm and giving. You make me
want to give you everything I am and have."

"Do you?" he murmured, shifting her under him

to imprison her under his body. "Do you want to give me everything?"

"Everything..." Jackie assented on a sigh of passionate contentment. "Everything, Adam..." she repeated pleasurably, adjusting herself to his contours to derive every ounce of delicious contact she could.

"Say my name again," he whispered against her throat, replacing his mouth with his hand on her breast.

"Adam..." she breathed against his cheek, then feathered it with kisses, her lips soft and teasing and sensitive to his skin.

"Again..." he demanded, his breathing harshening.

"Adam..." she groaned, and then anticipating his demand for more, she cradled his face in her hands and lifted his head to stare with passion into his eyes. "Adam... Adam... Adam..."

Jackie would have repeated his name endlessly, but his lips captured hers in a swooping, demanding possession she met with eagerness while her body rose up to meet the pressure of his with total abandon.

There remained only the last step of their loving to take, but when Jackie mindlessly inserted her hands into the waistband of Adam's trousers, then attempted to move them to unfasten the irritating impediment to her complete satisfaction, Adam stopped her by wrapping his arms around her so tightly, she couldn't move.

"Adam... please..." Jackie pleaded softly against his ear.

"Shh..." Adam's strangled tone showed his difficulty in maintaining control. "You know we can't—not yet." His grip tightened slightly as the meaning of his words sank finally into Jackie's befuddled comprehension and stilled her movements. The tightening of his arms was a reassurance, a tender desire to comfort her in her frustration, an indication that he shared that frustration.

"Be still a moment," he whispered gently. "If you move before I get control, I'll never be able to stop...."

There was a curious quality to his statement, as though he were talking about forever instead of about this particular moment, and it pulled at Jackie's heart, giving her the strength to obey him instead of her body.

For long moments they lay locked together, savoring with exquisite torture the reduction of their passion, slowly...slowly...until their breathing quietened and their taut muscles gradually relaxed.

At last Adam made the effort to raise himself, to brace himself on his elbows and to take her face into his gentle palms. He stared down at her with emotion deepening his eyes to brown, their expression caressing and wondering, yet cautious as well—and terribly serious. "You're getting to me, Jack," he said softly. "I feel like I'm on the edge of a cliff and that if I don't pull back, I'm going to fall head over heels...with no chance of ever getting back."

Jackie matched his seriousness, her eyes tenderly blue, luminous with the remnants of passion, questioning gently what he wanted her to say.

"Am I a fool if I take that next step?" he asked her

with quiet vehemence. "Do you want me to?" His eyes searched hers. "Do you want to?"

When Jackie didn't answer immediately, taking the time she needed to make such a momentous decision, Adam expressed the basis of his doubts. "I think you're worth the danger, Jack," he whispered softly. "The question is, do you think I am? Am I going to be able to compete with Matt?"

Jackie's eyes widened as she stared back at the serious inquiry in Adam's, and her answer came without volition. "Of course you are. Of course you can." And because she had spoken spontaneously, and because of the certainty in her heart when the words came out, she knew them to be true.

The knowledge was like a burst of sunshine after months of rain. Surprise, then happiness, shone from her eyes and creased her lovely swollen-with-kisses mouth into a radiant smile.

After a momentary hesitation while Adam studied that look and that smile, he seemed to relax all at once, and his own firmly tender mouth curved into a satisfied smile. "So we're going to step out together, hmmm?" he said on a deep note of tender amused emotion.

Jackie nodded, then threw both arms around Adam's neck to squeeze him tight to her for a long moment before she drew back and planted a smacking kiss on his mouth. Beaming at him, confident in a renewed future, she asked almost complacently, "So now what do we do?"

Adam eyed her consideringly for a moment while he thought, then with a certain reluctance that was enormously satisfying to Jackie, he lifted himself into a sitting position. "Now we learn each other," he pronounced with wry self-mockery, looking down at Jackie with lifted eyebrows. When she looked puzzled, he elaborated. "We know the passion's there." And with a rueful grin, he drawled, "Isn't it?"

"It is. Oh, yes, it *is*." Jackie nodded affirmatively, her look ludicrously solemn.

Adam reacted with amused, self-confident male pleasure, but then he was back to seriousness. "Now we need to know if we're compatible. And as hard as it is for me to say this, I think we ought to play down the sexual attraction while we learn if we've got what it takes to make the rest of our relationship work."

Jackie's frown displayed her aversion to his suggestion, but Adam was adamant. "Jack, if I take you to bed now, I'm never going to be able to stop. You're like an addictive drug in that respect. Once you hook me, you hook yourself, because I won't let you go. Can you understand that?"

Jackie solemnly shook her head no. In her view the physical thing between them should be expressed and allowed to enhance the rest of what was between them.

Adam sighed, then shrugged. "You might as well learn this about me right now, Jack. I've got a ruthless streak a yard wide. I'm trying to overcome it where you're concerned so that we don't make a mistake. But once I've tasted all of you, once the addiction takes hold, there isn't anything I won't do to keep you. Don't play with fire," he advised her with a hard warning look that showed Jackie he was entirely serious and entirely capable of carrying out his threat. "I know myself. Take my word for it and protect yourself until you're sure you're committed. Because once I am, I'll take your commitment whether you want to give it or not."

Jackie blinked a little at that, realizing that she really didn't know Adam all that well, and suspecting that he was a great deal more formidable than she had thought. His strong will might be covered up generally by his humor and gentleness, but it was there, all right. Still, it was heartwarming that he was trying to warn her—that he was capable of subduing what he obviously wanted so strongly for her sake.

"All right, Adam. If that's what you want, we'll do it your way," she finally agreed, though reluctantly. "But it isn't going to be easy...." She gave him a half-petulant look that expressed her irritation at having to subdue her natural inclinations.

Adam grinned wickedly, reaching down a hand to run his thumb over Jackie's swollen lips. "No, it isn't going to be easy," he agreed with rueful amusement. "Especially since this is the first time in my life I've ever come up against a woman who doesn't want to take no for an answer. Usually it's the other way around, I believe," he teased solemnly.

"Huh!" Jackie responded, flushing a little at Adam's reference to her unbridled sensuality. "I'll bet! You can't tell me no woman has tried to seduce you before this, Adam Clarke!"

Adam looked innocently naive. "Was that what

you were trying to do? Seduce me?'' he asked in a prim tone. "You animal!'' He gave a shudder of pretended anger.

"Oh, shut up!'' Jackie said with real disgust, pushing him away so that she could sit up. "It was the other way around, remember? You're the one who came charging around that table like a bull in heat!''

Adam pretended to wince at her earthy description, but when Jackie started to stand up, he grabbed her around the waist and pulled her down onto his lap, laughing at her ineffectual protests. They tussled for a few moments before Jackie let him win the battle and settled down against him in contentment to be sheltered in his arms.

"Are we going to play house, then?'' she asked musingly, and then at Adam's stern look at her, she said with dry resignation, "Leaving out the bedroom part, of course.''

"Exactly,'' Adam said, his own tone dryly resigned. "We practice being married to see if we're going to be able to get it right and start a real marriage.''

"Well, in that case,'' Jackie said in a bored tone, stifling an elaborate yawn, "I think I'll go to bed.'' She looked at Adam innocently. "I have a headache, dear, so if you wouldn't mind sleeping alone tonight...''

Adam's expression grew mock ferocious. "No wife of mine is going to be *allowed* headaches at bedtime, woman. We might as well get that straight right now!''

Jackie got to her feet, idly waving a hand in dismissal. "Promises, promises,'' she scoffed as she slunk toward the bedroom, managing to look dejected. "I can see already I'm going to have to open an account at an erotic clothing store just to get your attention."

Adam stifled a laugh, but when he spoke, his tone was deadly serious. "I think the sort of garments you have in mind might look a little ridiculous on a pregnant woman, don't you?"

That stopped her. Jackie swung around to stare at Adam wide-eyed. "Huh?" Her ineloquent reaction gave little indication that she made her living as a writer who supposedly had an extensive vocabulary.

"Well," Adam replied with elaborate casualness. "I'd judge you to be around thirty years old, am I right?" After Jackie's bristling nod, he shrugged magnanimously. "Then if you're going to have children, don't you think you'd better get to it? Older women, statistically—"

He got no further, as Jackie attacked. "I'm seven years younger than you, buster! You're the one who'd better get to it!" she yelled defensively.

Adam smiled sweetly at her. "My point exactly," he said. "Although I'm not the one who will have to carry the child, and I believe it's the health of the mother that is of more importance," he crowed with infuriating superiority.

Jackie was incoherent with rage for a moment before she realized that Adam's eyes were fairly dancing with mischievous amusement at having provoked her again. Then, with a mighty effort, she clamped down on her temper and smiled a saccharine smile. "How right you are, dear Adam," she cooed at him simperingly. "But I believe there's a biological function that has to take place before a child can be conceived...."

Her expression then grew ferociously thunderous. "And at this rate, we're going to have a trial divorce before we ever get started on our so-called trial marriage!" With that she turned on her heels, marched into her bedroom, and slammed the door behind her with a satisfying thump, even as she heard Adam's laughter bubbling toward her with unmitigated glee.

Chapter Eight

Jackie woke the next morning to the familiar snick of the drawer that signaled Adam was up to his usual predawn rummagings, only this time Jackie kept her eyes shut and forced herself to breathe deeply and naturally as though she were still asleep. It was hard, especially in view of the fact that she desperately longed for a repetition of the previous morning's pleasurable awakening at Adam's hands. However, in view of his proscription against any sexual involvement between them for the time being, she thought it far safer to avoid temptation.

"Good morning, Jack." The soft words made her jerk convulsively, and a second later she heard Adam's soft chuckle. "I thought you were awake," he murmured with satisfied complacency. "I could feel it."

"How could I help it." She began a groggy complaint, and then choked it off at Adam's warning look. Switching tactics with the speed of light, she managed a feeble smile and an approximation of polite sincerity. "Good morning, Adam," she said with a mental gnashing of teeth.

Adam looked at her sharply, then relaxed his features into a rueful grin. "I'm a better teacher than I thought," he murmured with quiet humor. "Or else you're a bigger coward than I realized." He reached down and tousled her hair, then padded to the door on bare feet. "I'll put the coffee on and let you have the bathroom first," he said from the threshold. "I almost didn't get out of your way in time yesterday, and I'm too young to be trampled under the heels of a beautiful woman." With another chuckle he was gone, and Jackie sighed, groaned, then hauled herself out of bed. It was plain she was going to have to get used to being a morning person since Adam had entered her life, she thought groggily as she pulled on her robe and fumbled her way to the bathroom. But at least he showed signs of being a considerate housemate. It hadn't taken him long to learn that the bathroom was her first priority upon arising.

That day set the pattern for several days to come. Adam would waken her, get breakfast, pack himself a lunch, and depart for his hunting. He switched his bathing to the evening after coming in tired and dirty—and without a deer, Jackie noted with some puzzlement—and Jackie would have dinner timed for when he was clean, relaxed, and in a mood for it. After eating, they would sit companionably together and talk, trying to explore everything about each other that mattered, or play cards, until one or the other of them elected for bed. Usually it was Jackie who elected for bed, because she was finding it increasingly impossible to spend very much time with Adam before his very physical nearness began to drive her almost insane with the desire to touch him. It didn't help her ego a bit when Adam didn't seem to have near as much difficulty keeping his hands off her as she did in keeping hers off him.

She spent her days working on her book, amazed at the smooth flow of it and even more amazed at its content. Without volition she seemed to be using the writing as a means of working out her own conflicts about Matt and Adam, and Adam was unquestionably emerging as the winner in the bizarre rivalry. Couched as fiction, the narrative was no more than a thinly veiled recapping of her life with Matt, the love and tenderness she felt for him, the accidents following his death, and increasingly, her willingness to let him go. Then Adam simply took over the book. Of course, his part was three-fourths fantasy, since he wasn't giving her much scope for erotic passages, she thought somewhat grumpily. However, her emerging feelings for him came through loud and clear, and it was for that reason that Jackie hid her manuscript away from his discerning eyes.

Her reasoning was simple. She was quite aware she was falling in love with Adam, but she was also painfully aware that Adam was giving her no clues as to his own emotions. He was unfailingly kind, humorous, thoughtful, pleasant to be with, and considerate, but for all the interest in her as a woman he was showing, she might as well have been sixty years old, dumpy, grandmotherly, and totally unexciting. She wasn't about to take the chance of his reading what she'd written and discovering he had her in the palm of his hand emotionally and spiritually as well as physically.

Each day she made time to take a walk and explore her surroundings further, striking out in a different direction periodically. But while the area was beautiful whichever way she took, she found herself returning again and again to the clearing she had initially discovered, though she had not yet taken a whole day to picnic and explore the area at the bottom of the waterfall as she had promised herself, and she was uncomfortably aware that her recalcitrance sprang from a reluctance to leave her ever more fascinating book, in which she could order her relationship with Adam to her own specifications.

That thought struck one day as she was returning to the cabin to beat an approaching rainstorm, and whether it was from the dark, gloomy weather or from the realization that it looked very much as though Adam were having second thoughts about deepening their relationship, she suddenly found herself feeling depressed. The trial marriage, while thoroughly delightful in the sense of getting to know and care for Adam more and more each day, was becoming unbearably stressful from the point of being unable to touch him, to utter teasing, tender, provocative words of love—to act naturally, in short.

By the time she reached the cabin, with the rain spattering its first drops on her skin, she was gloomily looking forward to a hot drink and a nap, which was a sure sign something was amiss, as she never napped. As she scurried up the steps she faltered at seeing

Adam's disreputable pickup parked off to the side in its usual spot.

Damn the man! she thought with irritable forceful-ness. Had the weather forced him to give up his hunt-ing? Was she going to be trapped with him inside the cozy cabin with a storm raging outside? she thought. How unfortunate! This sort of weather always made her feel romantic—in need of the security of her loved one's arms, the tempest outside sparking her to an inner tempest that Matt had enjoyed to the point where, if at all possible, he would come home to her during storms. She had always welcomed him with open arms, but Adam's arms weren't open, and she didn't know how she was going to be able to keep from exercising an overpowering desire to force them so.

After scouting the main room quickly and discover-ing that Adam was not in evidence, Jackie hung up her Windbreaker and discarded her damp shoes, wondering crossly where he could be. The bathroom was empty as well, its door open when not in use as had become their habit, since it didn't have a lock and there was always the danger of their walking in on each other.

That left the bedroom, and since its door was closed, and she distinctly remembered leaving it open, she thought she'd hit pay dirt. But why would Adam be in her bedroom with the door closed? she wondered. She felt a dart of real fear as she remem-bered that her book was deposited in its usual place under the bed, the only suitable hiding spot she had been able to find for it. But surely Adam wouldn't invade her privacy by reading it, even if he had accidentally found it! she hoped.

Like hell he wouldn't, she thought with angry dismay as she crossed the room to fling open the door of the bedroom, prepared to wage a battle royal if he had dared do such a thing.

She gave a small gasp as she saw Adam sprawled on the bed, taking up a good two thirds of its surface with his large frame and snoring gently as he lay sleeping in deep contentment, one arm cuddling a pillow, the other stretched out beside him. He was fully dressed, lying on his stomach, his dark hair endearingly tousled and his stockinged feet protruding over the end of the bed a few inches, attesting to the fact that a standard mattress was never meant for someone his size.

Jackie stifled a relieved giggle and couldn't resist creeping to the side of the bed to gaze down at him with amused fondness, which quickly turned to a wrench of longing to lie down beside him and be enfolded into those strong arms and feel the length of him against her. *Lord, you're in bad shape,* she chided herself with wry sadness. *This man can't even take a nap near you without you wanting to crawl into bed with him. Have you turned into one of those widows men always assume to be "ready"?* Only, she knew with a despairing certainty that had it been any other man than Adam lying there, she would have felt nothing like the wild heat that was coursing through her veins at this instant.

She turned a groan of desire into a sigh of resignation and went on tiptoe to the closet to gather up a blanket to cover Adam. The room was chilly, and though she knew men usually generated more body heat than women, it wouldn't improve matters as they stood now if Adam caught cold and couldn't go out hunting for a few days. Besides the frustrating prospect of having him around to moon over, he was probably like most men and would make a federal case out of a small illness, while bearing a major one stoically.

She draped the blanket over him as lightly and delicately as possible, trying not to waken him, and was about to turn away when his hand came up like lightning to grasp her arm and pull her down in a heap onto the bed.

"Adam," she gasped in indignation as she struggled against his efforts to pull her down next to him. "I thought you were asleep."

Adam smiled with lazy wickedness as he easily subdued her struggle and pulled her under the blanket with him, thrusting a leg and an arm over her body to hold her still. "I was. Hold still, you're pulling the blanket off my other side. But you woke me up with your tender ministrations." He increased the pressure of his arm and leg and frowned at her continued flounderings with mild annoyance. "Damn it, Jack, be still! I'm not trying to rape you, I only want to get close to you."

Adam's words had the effect of making her cease her struggles and gaze up at him in astonishment. "That's better," he said with sleepy satisfaction as he calmly arranged the blanket to cover the side where Jackie had pulled it away.

Jackie felt a little as though she had wandered into a live action dream as Adam tucked her more comfortably against him and rested his head against hers, then gave a wide yawn and closed his sleepily seductive eyes, giving every indication he intended to go to sleep again. God, she thought a little wildly, she had known Adam was prone to the unexpected, but this was the limit! If he thought she was going to lie here and suffer the pangs of the damned from wanting him while he snoozed away in comfort, he had another think coming!

"Adam?" she asked with a grim but reasonable patience. "Are you intending that we take a nap together?"

Adam nodded his head slightly and gave a muffled "Ummm..." in a tone consistent with a man who was impatient to get back to sleep.

"Why?" There was a rising note of strangulated incredulity in her voice, but still she managed to keep her voice down and her patience intact.

"Want company..." Adam mumbled indistinctly, rubbing his head against hers and tightening his arms fractionally before relaxing again into a posture of sleep.

Jackie blinked and stared up at the ceiling, aware from the tempo of Adam's breathing that already he was out like a light. He had her imprisoned so tightly, however, there was no way she could get loose, even though he was unconscious. There wasn't a thing she could do.

She reflected upon the matter, noting how warm Adam's body felt against hers, how cozy and comfortable the bed felt under her and the blanket over her, and how good the sound of thunder and the splash of rain against the window was when you were hearing them from the sanctuary of a man like Adam's arms. The only fly in the ointment was the curl of desire she felt enveloping her from the tip of her head to her toes; but it was only a curl, not a raging current, since Adam's unconscious state precluded letting out all stops.

Oh, what the hell, she decided all at once, a yawn overtaking her in midthought. *This is the best you've felt in months. Stop spoiling it for yourself. Enjoy! Enjoy!* With a contented little smile she snuggled more closely against Adam and proceeded to do just that until she drifted off into a real dream that was almost as good as reality.

Sometime later she woke to the feel of Adam's hand stroking her back with long, soothing, delicious movements, and she was smiling before she opened her eyes. She had her head on his shoulder, her leg thrown over his thighs, and her arm thrown across his chest possessively. It was the best awakening she could remember since her days with Matt.

"Sleep good?" Adam's lazy query seemed the most natural thing in the world to her ears.

"Ummm-hmmm..." She yawned and settled back against him.

"Me, too." There was a smile in his voice and satisfaction, as well. "There's only one more thing I want to make this a perfect afternoon," he added softly.

"Whazzat?" Jackie mumbled in sleepy contentment.

"I want to make love to you."

Every sense came alert at once, bells started ringing in Jackie's head, her heart began pumping blood at express speed, a trembling seized her limbs, and her breath stopped dead in her throat.

Adam must have felt her reaction, but his movements were slow and calm, deliberately casual, as he turned her face up to his and brushed his lips against hers. Jackie swallowed convulsively and through the greatest effort of will managed to say, "What about our agreement?" She swallowed again, adding, "What about a baby?"

Adam kissed her again, more lingeringly this time, then he drew back and whispered, "We'll stop short of both." His next kiss contained a purposefulness Jackie recognized and approved of wholeheartedly.

If she hadn't already known from her previous experiences with Adam, she would have discovered right then that making love was like riding a bicycle— once you had mastered it, you never forgot how. Adam had evidently graduated with honors, and judging from his responses to her enthusiastic participation, she was no slouch herself. And the nicest thing about it—if the word *nice* was the appropriate one to apply in a situation of this sort—was that what they were doing was, indeed, making love, not simply having sex.

Adam demonstrated exquisite instincts in the considerate tenderness with which he began, graduating shortly thereafter to masterful demands, and capturing Jackie's heart completely with the desperate struggle he waged to keep from taking her totally into his possession. She knew what he was going through, because she had her own struggle not to actively provoke him into disregarding chivalry and step over that fine line that grew closer with every touch, every murmur, every look they exchanged.

In the end they both demonstrated a high degree of creativity that, while not satisfying them emotionally the way the complete unity they both craved desperately would have, at least allowed an explosion of the tension they had excited in one another and enabled them to drift back into sanity relatively satisfied.

Afterward, Jackie lay in Adam's arms and felt tears of both gratitude and frustration moisten her eyes. She was grateful to have discovered finally and irrevocably that she was in love with Adam and that her life hadn't ended with Matt where her emotions were concerned. No matter how, or if, her relationship with Adam developed, she had had this much of him, and as soon as she could get into Pinedale without demonstrating unseemly haste, she intended to have even more, she knew. A town that size had to have a doctor, surely. If not, she'd drive all the way to Jackson.

Adam was silent for a long time. Finally, he raised himself to one elbow, caressed her breast with wondering possessiveness, and kissed her gently on the lips. "You're quite a woman, do you know that, sweet?"

Jackie smiled with languorous mischief and nodded complacently. "Yes, of course," she teased. "If you had asked me before, I could have told you." Her eyes glinted with suppressed humor as Adam gave her a mocking look that acknowledged her pretended conceit with a grain of salt. "And may I return the compliment," she said softly on a more serious note. "You're quite a man, Adam darling."

Then it was his turn to preen. "Of course. If you had asked me before, I could have told you," he echoed her words with a wicked grin. And then his grin faded and his expression sobered. "I think we had better do something about this situation, though— and fast. I'm not up to making a noble effort like that often. I'm not even sure that I haven't used up what little store of self-control I have already." He looked down at her with a seriousness and a hesitation that twisted her heart. "Are you willing—" He paused, obviously in a quandary about whether it was wise to suggest what he was about to. "Jack, I don't want to pressure you like this...involve you more seriously with me when you may not be ready...."

Jackie gazed at him with loving serenity. "I think it's too late to stop now, don't you, Adam? My control is not any more reliable than yours. I'd like to see a doctor tomorrow. Will that be soon enough, do you think?" she asked with an engaging smile.

Adam growled as he hugged her to him more closely. "Just barely," he muttered, and it was obvious he was strongly moved by her generosity and understanding. "But it won't be if I don't sleep in the living room tonight."

Jackie groaned at the thought and looked at him with reproachful protest. "Oh, Adam, no. I'll be good, I promise you. I won't move a muscle or say a word or—"

Adam cut her off with a hard kiss. "The hell you

won't!" he said with masculine forcefulness. "Do you think I ever want to see the day when you don't respond? Do you think I *want* to sleep in there?" He was grim with frustration, but then his look turned rueful. "The trouble is, *I* won't be good, and you know it."

Pleased by his confession, Jackie smiled generously up at him, then gave him a peck on the cheek and sat up. "Very well," she said with an exaggerated look of martyrdom. "You go right ahead and sleep another night on that floor. See how accommodating I can be?"

Adam pulled her down on top of him, laughing softly, and kissed her with every indication that he intended to begin making love to her again. But then he quickly rolled her off him and sat up. "For your information, I haven't *slept* on that floor for several nights," he informed her with wry self-mockery. "I've merely lain there suffering the pangs of adolescent heat for the lady in the next room. And I can tell you it wasn't pleasant, and I won't like it any more tonight than I have before. But I guess I can stand it this one last time, though it will be even harder after this afternoon."

He stood up and stretched his body in a powerful gracefulness that had Jackie's senses warming to life again most satisfactorily. He showed not the slightest embarrassment at standing before her in all his nude glory, and Jackie realized that she didn't feel any shame at her own nakedness, either, which gave her a contented sense of belonging and the sureness that she was right to love this man.

As Adam reached down to pick up his discarded clothing, the sight of it reminded Jackie she had better gather up such items as she and Adam needed washed and take them with her into Pinedale the next day to the Laundromat. There weren't any facilities for washing clothes at the cabin, and she was going to feel the need for clean clothes soon. She said as much to Adam, and he cocked an eyebrow at her, assuming a stance of chauvinistic arrogance.

"It's about time, woman," he intoned in a heavy, authoritative voice. "You've been slack in your duties, but kind as I am, I was waiting to mention it until things got critical."

Instantly falling into the spirit of the game, Jackie sat up and wrung her hands in a pleading, anxious gesture, looking up at Adam with wide appealing eyes. "Oh, sir, please forgive me," she said in a pitiful voice. "It's just that with scrubbing the floors, baking the bread, hauling in the wood—not to mention chopping it first—cleaning the windows, walking five miles to get groceries, and taking care of our ten children, it slipped my mind." She blinked imaginary tears away and moved to her knees to assume a posture of abject submission. "You won't—won't beat me again, will you?" she asked fearfully.

Adam made a gesture of regal dismissal, then patted his hand over his mouth as though concealing a bored yawn. "Not this time," he promised magnanimously. "Just don't let it happen again, wench. I'm a kind and patient man, but I'll only put up with so much from a mere female."

Jackie gave an exaggerated sigh of relief and reached

over to grab his hand, covering it with eager kisses. "Oh, thank you, thank you," she babbled gratefully. "I was so afraid you were going to break my arm again, and you remember how awkward it was to do all the work and carry the children one-handed."

Adam fixed her with a stern scowl. "Are you complaining?" he asked in a menacing voice.

Jackie let go of his hand and cowered down, covering her cheeks with her hands in woeful dismay, her eyes wide with horror. "Oh, God forbid!" she moaned, terror in her voice. "Never, never, never would I complain! Why, I was just thinking how clever you were to break my arm when, if you recall, it gave you such scope to find new ways of making love. You were so creative, and I can't wait to see what you come up with if you ever break my leg!"

Adam was choking with laughter by the time she got through with her babbling, and it was all he could do to play the rest of his part. "Well, then, get up from there, you lazy layabout," he ordered sternly. "I want my dinner!" He turned and marched regally to the door, where he turned to glower at her. "I want my usual sixteen courses, and I want them ready in fifteen minutes. See to it!"

Jackie was howling with laughter when, a second later, his grinning face peeked around the doorjamb, and in a meek voice that was totally incongruous with his bulk and air of authority, he said, "But if you can't see your way clear to fix sixteen courses, I'll settle for a sandwich."

"You'll get what I fix and like it, you nitwit!" Jackie responded between her gulps of laughter.

Adam gave a meek nod, but the grin was still there. "Yes, dear," he said, quietly submissive. "I'll go bathe and keep out of your way for a while."

And then he was gone, and Jackie wiped the tears of laughter from her eyes as she climbed out of bed to find a robe. She wanted a bath too, but she would wait until Adam was through, though the thought of joining him crossed her mind with wicked temptation, even though the tub was so small, she didn't know how Adam would manage to fold himself into it alone, much less try to accommodate her as well.

Jackie was on her way to the kitchen to fix Adam his sandwich when the thought struck her that ham and cheese was no way to celebrate what she was feeling. With the rain still pouring outside, it would be perfect to have that candlelight dinner she had hesitated over before, and candles called for something more spectacular in the way of a menu than sandwiches.

Humming happily as she rummaged through the refrigerator and the cabinets, Jackie decided on steak Diane flamed with brandy, spinach salad with sour cream and fresh mushrooms, and French rolls. There was nothing really fancy to be had for dessert, but she thought plain vanilla ice cream with Kahlúa over it would serve quite nicely.

Adam joined her as she was putting the finishing touches to the table, and his eyes were admiring as he noted her preparations. "Did I put the fear of God into you, woman?" he asked teasingly as he pulled her against him and wrapped his arms about her waist.

Jackie laughed and leaned back in his arms with her

hands on his shoulders. "No, darling. I just felt like celebrating. Do you mind?"

Adam shook his head, his expression unfathomable as he looked at the shining happiness in Jackie's eyes, the tender curve to her delectable mouth, and the tousled luxuriousness of her hair. "I can't imagine minding anything you might do," he said absently, his tone almost grave.

"Oh, ho?" she responded with a teasing smile and a glint of mischief in her eyes. "You're giving me carte blanche, then?"

For a moment she didn't think he was going to respond in a light vein, but then he smacked her bottom lightly before releasing her. "Just so long as you remember who's boss," he said with a faint gruffness in his voice, returning briefly to the game they'd played earlier.

"I'm going to take my bath now," Jackie said with enthusiasm. "And I warn you, I'm going to dress for dinner, so if you don't want to appear to be a country bumpkin up against my dazzling sophistication, you'd better search out suitable attire to match my splendor." Then, at seeing Adam's slight frown in reaction to her words, Jackie reached up and caught his face between her hands, giving him a kiss of sweet acceptance that gave force to her next words. "Never mind, darling," she crooned softly. "I'd rather have you sitting across from me in overalls than Cary Grant in black tie and tails."

Adam caught her hands and kissed each palm in turn. His mouth was quirked with humor as he raised skeptical eyes to hers. "Liar," he said with soft mockery. "But I'm going to choose to believe you."

Jackie chuckled and swayed in an exaggerated model's walk across the room, pausing in the door of the bathroom to give Adam a sultry, smoldering, vampish look over her shoulder. Taunting him, she stuck out one hip and placed a fist on it, giving a slow bump and grind for a moment before turning gracefully on her heels. She entered the bathroom and shut the door most of the way but left her hand outside the panel to trail seductively down, giving a little flutter of her fingers, before closing the door with a soft click.

She could hear Adam's snort of laughter through the door, and she was grinning as she dropped her sexy pose and hurried to turn on the taps of the ancient bathtub.

Thirty minutes later, after taking particular care with her makeup and fastening her hair into the French knot she favored, she donned black velvet evening pants and a white silky off-the-shoulder blouse, thanking her stars she had brought them when there had seemed to be no earthly reason to do so. The effect was eye-catchingly sophisticated and sexy, and Jackie noted with pleasure that her figure seemed made for the outfit. She was not exceptionally tall, but she gave the illusion of having more height than she possessed by virtue of her slender straight posture. Her shoulders were smooth and feminine, and her breasts were firm and generous enough to be enticing without spoiling the elegant lines of her body.

Adam was standing by the fireplace, staring into the flames, when she emerged from her bedroom, and Jackie felt unaccountably nervous for a second as she waited for him to turn and notice her. Then his hazel eyes were holding her prisoner as he swept her up and down with an approving look.

He had on a white shirt that emphasized the breadth of his shoulders, dark pants, and no tie. Bless him, Jackie thought with welling tenderness tugging at her heart. Where had he gotten the shirt?

She felt her insides turn over as Adam walked toward her, his eyes eating her as he came, and then she was in his arms and he was kissing her with as much hunger on his lips as she had seen in his eyes. She was limp with desire by the time he lifted his head, and gasping for breath, but perfectly willing to stand there kissing Adam all night if that was what he wanted. What did breathing matter, anyway? Compared to the warm magic of Adam's firm, strong body against hers, his masculine scent, the expertise of his lips as they wrung every atom of response from hers, and the excitement of his hands on her hips, pressing her against him, breathing was a very minor consideration indeed.

"Wow!" she murmured on a gulp as she gazed with passion-clouded eyes into his slumbering, dominating ones. "You do know how to express appreciation for a lady's efforts, don't you?"

"Then the lady's not disappointed?" he murmured huskily as he dipped his head again to nibble the sensitive skin on her throat.

"Not in the least," she moaned with a shudder of arousal as she felt his moist tongue tasting her skin. "If I'd known I'd get this reaction, I'd have dressed up long before now."

Adam lifted his head and gave her a smoldering

look that put her earlier funning to shame, simply because he was sincere. "You don't have to dress up to get this kind of reaction from me," he said as he brushed her lips again. "I was ready for this the first time I saw you, braid, slippers, and all. If you hadn't had a gun on me, I might have tossed you into bed then and there."

Jackie pouted. "*Now* he tells me," she muttered wrathfully. "I *knew* I should have left that weapon at home."

Adam grinned lazily at her, kissed her again, then pushed her away with a great deal of reluctance. "Let that be a lesson to you," he mocked her gently. "You can catch more flies with honey than vinegar. Now, I wonder if that dinner of yours can compete with your appearance." He turned her toward the kitchen. "That will take some doing!"

Jackie preceded him into the kitchen, tossing a request over her shoulder. "Adam, would you pour the wine while I get the steak?"

Adam nodded and followed her into the kitchen. From then on the evening took on all the charm any two lovers could wish for. The steak was perfect, the wine smooth as nectar, the salad fresh and delicious, and the French rolls crispy on the outside, soft and warm and delicious on the inside. But they could have been eating sawdust for all Jackie noticed. She was concentrating exclusively on Adam, hardly tasting what she ate, content to feast on him.

They left the dishes for the morning, not wanting to spoil the mood by anything so mundane as soapy water and dish towels, and moved to the couch, Jackie feeling as though she were floating on a cloud. It was heaven to be able to behave as she had wanted to for days. She curled up beside Adam, resting her head on his shoulder, feeling the strong, warm security of his arm about her waist, and simply breathed in Adam, felt Adam, luxuriated in Adam, and thought about nothing but Adam.

For a while they simply watched the flames with sleepy contentment, satiated with food, wine, and the cozy intimacy of the cabin while the rain and wind raged outside. Jackie wanted to stay there forever and would have been quite happy had the moment been frozen for all time. But then Adam stirred, shifting her more comfortably in his arms, and murmured, "Am I going too fast with you, Jack?"

Jackie opened her eyes and blinked at him in confusion for a moment. She had thought everything was settled between them, but it seemed Adam was still plagued by doubts. She moved slightly to search his face with her eyes, sensing that this was an important moment in their developing relationship.

"No, Adam," she assured him with soft seriousness. "I'm not a child. I know what I'm doing."

His gaze was broodingly serious as he returned her look. "I tried to live up to the agreement," he said with a tone of almost self-disgust. "But when I woke up with you in my arms this afternoon, and you were so warm and feminine and beautiful..." He shrugged resignedly. "I don't seem to have any willpower where you're concerned."

Jackie cocked an eyebrow at him, patently skeptical. "It seems to me you've been doing admirably in the willpower department during the past few days. I was beginning to think you'd lost all interest.''

Adam looked surprised, then he grinned. "You'll never know what it cost me," he teased as he hugged her closer to him. "I knew if I touched you, I was lost. I knew if I spoke to you the way I wanted to, I was lost. So I just kept my distance."

"You certainly did!" Jackie avowed with a certain amount of asperity. "You almost froze me out completely."

Adam's look mocked her. "You weren't cold this afternoon," he murmured, turning her into his arms and beginning a one-handed exploration that had Jackie's insides turning to molten heat within seconds.

"That's not fair," she murmured with breathless self-righteousness. "You took me by surprise. I was hardly awake—" She caught her breath on a moan as Adam punished her by capturing her breast in his palm.

"Am I taking you by surprise now?" he mocked gently, feathering her neck with nipping erotic kisses.

"Ah...er...perhaps..." Jackie responded with weakening self-defense.

"You mean you didn't know, when you dressed up like this and fixed that candlelight dinner, that I might take it as an invitation to make advances?" he whispered, tracing her ear with a gentle evocative finger.

"It may have occurred to me...." Jackie admitted with lingering reluctance, but as she said this, she turned into his arms and arched against him, causing him to draw in his breath in a shudder of arousal.

"Then you'll have to take the consequences, won't you?" Adam muttered against her mouth, his voice deep with emotion, his hands molding her to his length before he covered the tempting softness of her lips with his own demanding mouth and forced her head back with the strength of his kiss.

When he finally raised his head, Jackie was reduced to unthinking involvement in her feelings for Adam, in the passion he had aroused with his hungry assault, and mindlessly she uttered the only words that held any meaning for her at the moment. "Oh, Adam, I love you so..." she breathed so softly, the words were scarcely audible. "I love you, Adam..." she repeated with wondering sincerity, gazing into his eyes so that she could see their expression when Adam returned her vow as she was certain he would.

Her shock was total when, instead, Adam drew back, his frown transforming his features into that of a stranger. Then the frown softened as he saw Jackie's wide-eyed faltering reaction, and he was gentle when he spoke. "Jackie, it's too soon for you to know that. This is exactly what I was afraid would happen if we let our physical attraction get out of hand."

For long seconds Jackie simply stared at Adam, feeling in turn rebuffed, then incredulous at having her very real feelings disbelieved, and finally grimly determined to make Adam see that he didn't have the only blueprint for relationships, simply because his sister had had a bad experience.

She pulled back slightly, ignoring Adam's slightly distressed expression and looked him right in the eye. "How do you know it's too soon, Adam?" she asked with hard-fought-for calm. "Do judges have a manual that spells out the time schedule for falling in love?"

An exasperated, slightly peeved look passed over Adam's strong features before giving way to tender concern. "Jackie, come on, now. We talked about this—"

"I'm aware of what we talked about," Jackie interrupted him without rancor. "I'm also aware you've never been in love—at least that's what you told me." She raised her eyebrows inquiringly, inviting him to dispute her.

Adam gave an impatient shrug. "I've been close," he said without relenting an inch in his certitude. "And a man doesn't have to fall off a horse to realize it can hurt."

"No," Jackie admitted, tongue in cheek. "But that man can never know *exactly* how it feels until it's happened to him, either, can he?" She didn't wait for an answer and took a deep breath before plunging on, knowing she was on dangerous ground. "And I have been in love before, Adam—after a two-day acquaintance, I might add—and I know exactly how it feels."

She watched warily as Adam reacted first with the anger she had been afraid of, then with puzzlement. "What do you mean after a two-day acquaintance?"

It was Jackie's turn to shrug. "I was in love with Matt within two days after meeting him, and he was in love with me. We were married less than a month later." She hesitated, not liking the storm clouds in Adam's eyes, but instinctively knowing they both somehow had to get over the hurdle of Adam's jeal-

ousy of Matt. "It was a happier marriage than that of
many people who know one another for years before
marrying." Her expression softened as she watched
Adam struggling with the jealousy her words had invoked. "Adam," she said softly, raising a hand to
stroke his cheek. "I assure you the feeling is unmistakable. I promise you I haven't confused it with sexual attraction."

Doubt and hope chased one another in Adam's
eyes, but before he could resolve what he was feeling,
another thought hit Jackie. "Of course," she said
with slow thoughtfulness, "no two people are alike. It
may be that I'm the one who's rushing you." She
searched his face, noting that he was frowning, and
felt a little dart of fear. Nevertheless, she was not prepared to avoid the issue. "Adam, I know what I feel.
But I can understand if you need more time. I sometimes get the feeling—"

She hesitated, and Adam prodded her, his tone a
little grim. "Yes? Go on."

Jackie shook her head, but she answered. "I think
sometimes you're afraid of love, Adam; that you
don't like anyone else having that kind of power over
you; that you might actually prefer a marriage with
the woman in Montana, simply because you would
always be in control as you aren't madly in love with
her." She raised her eyes to his, her own questioning
and slightly pleading. "Is—is that within the realm of
possibility, Adam?"

To her dismay Adam didn't answer. Instead he got
to his feet and went to lean a hand against the fire-

place mantel, his strong profile looking as though it were etched in stone against the dancing play of the flames.

A numb detachment enveloped Jackie as she looked at Adam's downcast head and heard the growing echoes of silence in the room. That silence had lasted too long. The evening—and perhaps her hopes for the future—were ruined. "What are you thinking, Adam?" she finally asked out of a desperate need to fill the silence.

Adam's jaw tightened, then he swung his head to look at her with piercing resolve. "I'm thinking that you don't know me very well if that's what you believe," he said gratingly. "Which only points up what I've said all along." He straightened up and turned his body to face her, placing his hands on his hips and looking for all the world like an intransigent, arrogant know-it-all. At least that was how he looked to Jackie, whose irritation, frustration, and hurt were growing by leaps and bounds. "Both of us need more time," he stated bluntly. "And I'm going to see that we have it."

Cold fury erupted in Jackie's breast at his assumption that he was the only one who knew how this courtship—trial marriage, burgeoning relationship, whatever one wanted to call it—should be conducted. "Fine," she grated out through clenched teeth as she jumped to her feet and started toward her bedroom. "You let me know when I have your approval to love you, won't you, Judge?" she asked with sarcastic meekness. "I'm just a pathetic, stupid layperson, after all. It takes a modern-day Solomon to sort out these complicated matters." She stopped at her bedroom door and shot him a baleful glare, the need for revenge at his having thrown her love back in her face overcoming her common sense. "I'm only glad Matt was a common mortal like me. He knew what he wanted when he saw it and he took it, and as a result we didn't waste a lot of time trying to do the right thing." She said the last few words with mincing sarcasm, ignoring the growing anger Adam was showing. "We did the right thing quite naturally," Jackie taunted, throwing caution to the winds. "And every second that added to our marriage is precious to me. I hope you don't live to be sorry that you have to ponder every action you take for aeons. Even a jury has to arrive at a verdict sooner or later."

And with that she stepped into her room and slammed the door behind her, fighting tears of mingled rage and hurt and shame that Adam Clarke could reduce her to the status of a rebellious adolescent so easily, it was all she could do to remember she was a thirty-year-old widow who supposedly had gotten over that sort of idiocy long ago.

Chapter Nine

The next morning, Adam, his manner thoughtful and remote, offered to accompany Jackie into town, but she refused, thinking each of them needed some time away from the other to think things over. At least that was what she told herself, but underneath the facade she adopted there was a fear that Adam had changed his mind about wanting to deepen their relationship. Indeed, she was afraid that he might not even be interested in making love to her, and who could blame him after her performance the previous night? she wondered miserably. Throwing Matt up to him like that had been the height of stupidity and insensitivity, and in the light of day she couldn't believe she had actually done such a thing.

Big mouth! she castigated herself scathingly. *You never did know when to shut up!* And to make matters worse, she hadn't even had the courage to apologize to Adam this morning. His manner had been so remote, she had been seized with another bout of resentful anger over his arrogant assumption that he had all the answers about love and relationships and how the two were to be conducted.

So what was she supposed to do now? she wondered glumly as she reached the outskirts of Pinedale. Should she still try to see a physician on the off chance that she was wrong—that Adam was only temporarily angry and would get over it and still be willing to make a go of things?

Jackie's lips tightened into a firm line of determination. Damn right she should! Adam Clarke, even with all his faults—and he had a number of them, she thought spitefully—was worth fighting for. *That woman in Montana could never make him as happy as I could!* Jackie reinforced her determination spiritedly. There were heights to be reached in a relationship that Adam was only beginning to experience and he would never have the chance if he married the woman from Montana.

As she drove slowly through the streets of Pinedale, searching for a public telephone, Jackie's eyes gleamed with the light of battle. The next time Adam lost control she intended to be ready for him.

Spotting a phone booth next to a gas station, Jackie pulled in, hopped out of her car, and darted into the booth to seize the telephone book and look up the name of a physician. The phone rang for what seemed an eternity before a woman's voice answered. "Doctor's office. May I help you?"

Jackie explained with brevity that she would like to make an appointment for that morning, but without saying why other than that it was a female matter.

"Is it an emergency?" the voice asked anxiously.

"No—*no*," Jackie replied with hurried reassurance, then wished she hadn't when she heard the dismaying news that the doctor was out of town on an emergency, and that the appointment would have to wait until Tuesday of the next week, as he was booked solid until then.

"But doesn't he have someone taking over for him while he's gone?" Jackie asked incredulously.

"Yes, but I'm afraid the other doctor is on vacation this week. It's hunting season, you know." The voice sounded apologetic, but Jackie felt so frustrated, she couldn't respond with more than a slight degree of politeness.

"What happens if there *is* an emergency with both of them gone?"

"Oh, we have an ambulance service with paramedics," the voice said reassuringly. "We'd take whoever it was to Jackson."

"Well, that's a relief," Jackie said with forlorn dryness. After a moment, she realized she was stuck and she had better grab the appointment on Tuesday before it was taken, too. Arrangements were completed, and Jackie hung up the phone and left the booth to return to her car, her shoulders slumping with despondency. Once inside, she sat with her head on her hand, then reached into the glove compartment to search for a cigarette. She had stopped smoking six months earlier but the present situation seemed to call for a temporary relapse.

There was a crumpled package with no more than three or four dry, stale cigarettes left in it, but she sighed with relief, feeling grateful for any slight favor by then. She lit one, coughed and grimaced at the strong taste, then sat thinking.

Fate wasn't being very kind to her lately, she reflected glumly. Was there a guardian angel at work? And if so, who was being protected? Adam or herself? she wondered.

The thought was sobering, and she tried to find something to feel optimistic about. Perhaps it was just as well there would be a few days to cool down. Adam had seemed so positive about wanting to deepen their relationship, but if he could change his mind after one little fight, he had a lot to learn about love. Was it possible the woman in Montana *was* more suited to Adam's temperament? That he would be happier with pablum than with curry? she asked herself.

Jackie took another puff of the cigarette, grimaced at the taste, and put it out. It would be easy to remain a nonsmoker if all cigarettes tasted so nasty. Sighing dejectedly, she started the car and began to look for a Laundromat, deciding she could think just as easily while the clothes washed as she could sitting here accomplishing nothing.

Eventually, she found what she was looking for, and within a short while she had washers filled, soap added, and had seated herself along one wall to wait until it was time to dry the clothes. She felt dispirited enough that she decided she didn't want to think, and she pulled out a paperback novel from her purse, hoping her concentration would hold up enough to let her forget Adam for a short time.

Her hopes proved overly optimistic, and after reading the first page for the third time and still not having a clue as to what she'd read, she closed the book and stared out the window abstractedly, watching as a few people scurried here and there on whatever errands they were intent upon.

She watched disinterestedly as a man clad in a western hat and jacket walked along the far side of the street, and just as he was about to turn the corner she sat up, her eyes rounded in astonishment. That couldn't be Adam! she thought.

Jackie hadn't been able to see his features, as the hat shielded his face, but that walk, that form, the way he carried his shoulders. Surely there couldn't be two men in the world who moved with that particular blend of grace and masculine self-confidence? she realized.

Unthinkingly, she surged to her feet, leaving her purse, the clothes, and all of her cleaning supplies unattended as she raced out the door of the Laundromat. She ran across the street and up to the corner, taking the turn in a skid, and was just in time to see the man disappear into a drugstore. As he went in his profile was clearly visible, and she was positive it was Adam.

With hands on her hips, her face stormy with emotion, Jackie stared at the empty storefront, reflecting angrily that Adam hadn't put up any argument at all when she had turned down his offer to accompany her into Pinedale, yet here he was, sneaking into town behind her back!

Turning sharply on her heels to return to the Laundromat, Jackie's mind seethed with angry questions. Was Adam so anxious to avoid her that he wouldn't even share a ride into town with her? And then an even more nasty suspicion entered her mind. The drugstore most likely had a telephone. Was Adam calling the woman in Montana? And if so, why? To make sure she would still be waiting for him when he returned home? she wondered.

Miserable at the last thought, Jackie nevertheless struggled to overcome it. As she sat back down in the Laundromat the fates seemed to conspire against her when she looked up and noticed for the first time that the room she inhabited also contained a telephone. For a moment she stared at it, feeling lonely, beset by doubts and in need of a comforting shoulder to cry on as well as the distraction of listening to something other than her own unanswerable questions. She thought of Dr. Chelski, then dismissed the idea of calling him. He would be so delighted she was getting involved with a man again, and he was so convinced she was such a catch, he would scoff at her insecurities. The only one she could think of who might be just the right person to talk to was calm, levelheaded, maternalistic Liv, and without another moment's hesitation Jackie fished in her purse for money, then headed for the telephone.

She thanked her luck when she was able to catch Liv between clients, and after a few moments of greeting and explanation, Jackie got to the point of her call. "Liv, I need some advice," she got out hesitantly, aware that she sounded as miserable as she felt.

"What's the matter, honey?" Liv replied with only a tinge of curious anxiety in her calm voice. "You know I'll be happy to help if I can."

Slowly at first, and then with increasing confidence, Jackie spelled out what had happened since she had arrived in Wyoming, finishing with the impasse she and Adam had arrived at the previous night.

"I don't know what to do, Liv," Jackie said mournfully. "It's the first time in my life I've ever met a man so stubborn and so—so principled!" Her tone made it sound as though Adam's principles were loathsome objects better off kept from the light of day. Then she grew irritated when she heard Liv's delighted chuckle coming over the line.

"It's not funny, Liv!" she said crossly. "I'm not used to throwing myself at a man, much less one I'm in love with, and having him treat me like a harebrained idiot who doesn't know her own mind! And have you ever heard of a man in this day and age who absolutely refuses to go to bed with a woman? It's—it's—unnerving!"

That comment sparked another burst of laughter from Liv that had Jackie scowling at the instrument in her hand. When Liv finally calmed down, Jackie asked witheringly, "Are you sure you're finished laughing, or would you like me to tell you the latest joke I've heard?"

With the remnants of a chuckle in her voice, Liv relented. "I'm sorry, honey," she said with fond amusement, "but you're such an idiot!"

"An idiot?" Jackie burst out. "In what way?" And before Liv could answer, she muttered, "And if I am, it's not surprising. That man is enough to scramble *your* equilibrium much less mine."

"I'm not sure that's a compliment," Liv returned

wryly before getting to her point. "I just meant that this Adam of yours is obviously head over heels in love with you. You said it yourself. What man in this day and age *would* exercise such restraint unless he had your best interests in mind, and his own, as well? He told you flat out that you had the power to hurt him, and only love has that kind of power. And he told you why he's behaving as he is. What do you want, a signed affidavit that the man is a responsible, loving paragon in a world of shallow, self-centered hedonists?"

Frowning, aware that a faint sense of optimism was stirring in her mind, Jackie shrugged unconsciously. "I know he's special, Liv," she said quietly. "I wouldn't be in love with him if he weren't."

"Exactly," Liv responded with satisfaction. "So why are you calling me long distance to find out what you already know? Ten to one, Adam is on his way back to the cabin right now, eagerly awaiting his chance to do what he's wanted to do all along and couldn't."

A little moan escaped Jackie as she contemplated chances lost. "He still can't," she said disconsolately. "I couldn't get in to see the doctor, remember?"

With a hardheaded practicality that Jackie privately considered slightly hardhearted as well, Liv quipped, "So, it's back to creative loving for a while. So what? Just be patient, Jackie. Your man isn't going to run away. I'd stake my life on it."

"I'm not sure I would," Jackie responded with pessimism, but even under her halfhearted protest she felt better than she had when she'd called Liv, and she told her so. Liv laughed warmly.

"I'm glad I could help, honey," she said affectionately. "You mark my words. The next time you call me, it will be to tell me you're getting married. That man is hooked whether you believe it or not—as hooked as you obviously are."

"You really think so?" Jackie asked, her tone brightening slightly.

"I really think so," Liv answered with wry soberness. "And it couldn't have happened to a nicer guy, in my opinion, even though I don't know him yet. Or to a more deserving woman. I'm so relieved to know you've found someone again. You weren't meant to be alone."

Impulsively Jackie answered with a thought that had crossed her mind frequently since she had come to know Liv. "Neither were you, Liv. You'd make the most fantastic wife imaginable. I don't understand why—" She broke off, appalled at seeming to pry. If Liv had ever wanted to share her private thoughts on that subject, she would have done so long ago.

Liv handled the breach easily, only a trace of sadness in her tone. "Not me, kid. I'm spread too thin as it is. I made a commitment long ago to my job. I've yet to meet the man who would be willing to come second."

Jackie thought of Adam instantly, knowing without a doubt that *he* certainly wouldn't tolerate such an arrangement. "Okay, Liv." She dropped the subject. "Thanks again for your support. You're the best of friends."

"I try," Liv said easily, and then the two of them rang off.

A few moments later, as Jackie was folding Adam's clean, dry clothing, she forced herself to think calmly. So what if Adam had driven into town on his own? Maybe he had remembered something he needed after she'd already left the cabin. There could be any number of reasons why he was here on his own, and it was none of her business what they were—not yet, at least, she thought.

Her mood suffered another setback, however, when upon stopping at a grocer for fresh milk, bread, and vegetables, she ran straight into John Reardon and his peppery little wife, and from their identical expressions she discerned that they had somehow become aware that she and Adam were sharing the cabin and, furthermore, that they disapproved of the arrangement.

"Miss Roth!" Mrs. Reardon greeted her with a stern glance and a sniff that spelled out clearly the older woman's poor opinion of a female who would live with a man without benefit of marriage. "How's Judge Clarke?"

The tone of the question made Jackie aware that while Mrs. Reardon disapproved of her female tenant, she considered her beloved Adam as an unwilling victim rather than the instigator of the whole arrangement.

"He's fine," Jackie replied flatly, her back put up by the demonstration that the double standard was alive and well in Pinedale, Wyoming.

Mrs. Reardon opened her mouth to say more, but her husband broke in with a question of his own. "Did he say how the...er...mix-up about the cabin happened?" he asked, scratching his sparsely covered scalp in perplexity. "I didn't dream that call from his secretary, did I?"

Jackie shrugged, anxious to get away from this particular inquisition. "He seemed to think there hadn't been any such call," she said offhandedly.

Mrs. Reardon then spoke up again. "Annie tells us the two of you are engaged," she said with a suspicious inflection. "Happened mighty sudden, didn't it?"

Fed up, Jackie smiled sweetly at the other woman, even as she started moving her cart toward the checkout counter. "True love is like that sometimes, Mrs. Reardon," she said blithely, blinking her eyes innocently. "It just strikes like lightning. You know Adam." She tinkled a laugh at the glowering woman. "He's so virile and dynamic, he swept me off my feet."

With that she left the couple staring after her and swept to the counter to pay for the articles she'd bought, her calm visage giving no hint of the turmoil seething inside her. Then she drove swiftly back to the cabin in a mood to get things straightened out between them once and for all. She had to make Adam see that she knew her own mind.

Jackie was so immersed in thinking up what to say to Adam that she failed to note his pickup was missing from its usual spot, and it was not until she entered the cabin that she realized he wasn't back yet. Her temper returned in full force when she read the brief note he'd left her. It was so brief as to seem curt, and all it said was, "Gone hunting."

Damn Adam! Jackie's thoughts were hot with resentment. He was really chomping at the bit to make love to her, wasn't he? Oh, yes! He was so eager, he had to take himself off to Pinedale and then lie about where he'd gone. In her hotheaded anger Jackie completely forgot that making love was still not feasible, considering that she hadn't been able to see the doctor, and she muttered furious imprecations upon the absent Adam's head as she tossed his clean clothing any which way onto the bed, stomped back to the car to unload the groceries, carried them to the kitchen, and then practically threw them into the refrigerator and the cupboards. She punctuated her displeasure with generous slammings of any doors that came to hand and then stood in the middle of the room, wondering what else she could do to work off her temper.

Suddenly feeling claustrophobic shut up in the tiny cabin, she grabbed her jacket and left for a walk, thinking that by the time she had put a few miles behind her, she would feel more like talking to Adam than biting his head off.

Without conscious thought she found herself embarking upon a journey to the waterfall she had earlier promised herself she would revisit, and by the time she got there the exercise had cooled her temper and lightened her mood enough that she decided to descend to the bottom of the cliff to explore further.

Experiencing a slight sense of adventure, she eased herself over the edge and felt her way down over loose dirt and scattered rocks, skirting the huge boulders that barred her way. Occasionally, she came across a small tree valiantly struggling for a foothold on the slope, and she was grateful more than once for the handholds they afforded when she paused to catch her breath and get her bearings.

At last she reached the bottom, all traces of her earlier unhappiness having disappeared in the process of using her muscles and concentrating on the beautiful country around her. Her delight in the lovely clear green of the river water as it rushed over scattered rocks and boulders filled her senses, and she walked along the bank, luxuriating in the peaceful surroundings, enjoying the sense of being alone in a primeval world.

Eventually, she retraced her steps to sit for a long time on a large boulder overlooking the river, locked in a somnambulant peace, until the splash of a fish broke her torpor and reminded her that it was getting late. With a sigh of satisfaction at what the afternoon had held for her after its ignominious beginnings, she got up and walked back the way she had come, feeling a little dismayed at how far she had to climb to get back.

She was about a third of the way up and already feeling the strain in her legs and shoulders when she froze at the sound of a large rock breaking loose from its precarious hold on the cliffside and beginning to crash its way toward her. Flinging up her head with eyes widened in shock and fear, she gave a small scream and flung herself to the side, out of the pathway of the descending rock and the debris that came with it. Her sudden movement on the steep slope started a minor avalanche of its own, and Jackie tumbled over and over on a sidewise slant back down the cliffside.

Finally, with a painful, slapping thud to her stomach, a thin, supple sapling stopped her downward progress, and for long moments Jackie lay where she was, gasping for breath and thanking God that she had once again somehow managed to cheat death. She had heard the distant crash of the boulder as it landed at the bottom, and she could picture all too clearly what it would have been like to have stayed in its path.

When she regained her breath, she sat up slowly and painfully to assess the damages. Her jacket and slacks had protected her body somewhat, but she still had plenty of scrapes and scratches, and her whole body felt like one gigantic bruise. The thing that concerned her most, however, was the throbbing, agonizing ache in her right ankle, and even as she watched, it seemed to be swelling in size.

It was obvious she wasn't going to be able to walk on that leg, and with tears of pain and frustration in her eyes, she began to crawl up the slope, favoring the ankle, and from time to time casting anxious glances up at the darkening sky. Adam would be missing her by now and would be worried, of course, but though she was certain he would look for her, there was no guarantee he would look in the right direction. Therefore, it was up to her to get as far as possible on her own.

By the time she pulled herself, shaking and exhausted, over the edge of the cliff, her hands were shredded and she didn't want to think about the shape her knees must be in. She collapsed at the top, panting for breath, every muscle aching and her stomach heaving with nausea. She couldn't afford to give in to her misery, however. It was already dusk, and she had a long way to go still.

Pulling herself to a sitting position, she began to look around for a strong limb to use as a cane so that she could hobble upright, and when she finally found one, she gave a sob of relief as she got to her feet. It was a relief to be upright again, though even with the help of the stout limb, every step she took was fiery agony, and she couldn't help the tears that streamed down her face or the occasional sob that shook her shoulders as she clenched her teeth and plodded slowly onward.

Jackie was pale with exhaustion by the time she reached the familiar clearing with the brook and the pool and she sank down to rest on the rock. Lying back, she wiped her tears from her face, then collapsed, every muscle limp and hurting, her ankle a white flame of torment. She rested a long time, and when she roused again it was fully dark, and a growing chill in the air had her shivering beneath her light jacket.

The first step was enough to convince her she wasn't going to be able to walk anymore. With a cry of pain she crumpled to the ground and lay gritting her teeth against the waves of knifelike agony shooting through her ankle. Finally, they dwindled to bearable proportions, and with the last shreds of her strength she began a slow crawl down the trail that would lead her to safety, warmth . . . and Adam.

Her mind was closed to all but her own private hell,

and at first the faint call coming from a distance made no impression on her. At being forced to rest for a moment, she finally became aware of it, and with a sob of hope she gathered her strength to return the call. She put all the force she could muster into screaming the one word that meant anything at all to her at the moment. "Adammm!..."

The cry was a plea from her heart, and it took everything she had and more to accomplish. Afterward, she slumped to her side and lay at the edge of awareness, waiting, longing, for Adam to find her.

Surrounded by a haze of semiconsciousness, Jackie could hear nothing. The dim call from before seemed to be imagined. She was aware only of her bruised hands, stinging from her crawl down the path. Her progress had not been great, but there was no reserve of strength in her aching body to propel her onward. Her thoughts centered on Adam, the strong, confident man she loved, who would be searching for her and who would any minute walk into the clearing with sure steps and rescue her in his arms.

As if in a dream, a figure appeared in front of her, but its gait was unsteady. The person appeared to be searching frantically. As the figure approached, Jackie could discern dark male features. It was Adam. With a last breath she called out to him.

"Jack! Jack, what happened?" There was such tenderness underlying Adam's otherwise ferocious tone that Jackie felt a brief surge of bemused satisfaction along with the overwhelming relief of feeling Adam's arms around her at last. She couldn't speak as he cuddled her against the warm strength of his chest before lifting her into his arms to carry her back to the cabin. With a contented sigh she let herself drift into a painless sleep nestled in Adam's arms and only came blinking awake at the sound of his boots echoing on the wooden porch of the cabin. She winced slightly as he shifted her in his arms to open the door, then gave a groan of relief a moment later as he placed her gently on the couch.

Jackie watched in exhausted silence as Adam began to examine her for injuries, his face taut and grim with worry. "I'm all right," she managed to croak at him, grimacing then at the sound of her own voice. "Could I have some water, Adam?"

Without a word, Adam got to his feet in one smooth motion, strode to the kitchen for the water, and then she heard his impatient steps returning. "Here." His face looked haggard and his lips formed a grim line as he supported her back while she drank the whole glassful with thirsty eagerness. Then he took the glass, set it on the floor, and fixed her with an intimidating look.

Thinking quickly, wanting to avert the words of censure she was certain were coming, Jackie said hastily, "My ankle is in bad shape, Adam. Will you look at it?"

His frown disappearing to be replaced by a look of concern, Adam moved quickly to her feet and gently pushed her slacks above her ankle so that he could look at the swelling. Jackie bit her lip to cut off the gasps of pain as Adam probed with gentle fingers that were nevertheless instruments of torture.

"I'm sorry, Jack," Adam murmured as he flashed

her a look of apology at having to hurt her and saw the paleness of her skin and the weary agony in her eyes. She thought he meant his apology sincerely, but it didn't stop him from continuing his examination, and by the time he was done she had very nearly passed out as a result of his efforts.

"You haven't broken it," Adam pronounced finally. "Let's get you into a tub of hot water and assess the rest of your damages."

He was on his feet, striding toward the bathroom, before she could protest, and seconds later she heard the rusty taps of the tub being turned and the gush of water splashing into the tub. Adam was back almost immediately, his hands reaching to undo the buttons of her blouse. He unfastened them with sinfully efficient ease, and Jackie cocked an eyebrow at him and attempted a weak joke.

"You do that so well," she said smilingly. "Had a lot of practice, have you?"

A muscle was twitching in Adam's jaw, and his eyes reflected absolutely no humor to match her own half-hearted effort as he flashed her a glance fairly sparking with some emotion Jackie couldn't define but which chased cold chills down her back. Adam was displaying a facet of his character she hadn't known existed, and she was not at all happy to learn of its existence. He looked capable of anything at the moment, as though he were struggling hard to keep a rein on whatever emotion consumed him.

Jackie fell silent as he deftly, gently disposed of every stitch of her clothing, then picked her up and carried her to the bathroom. The water was deliciously hot once she got over the first flinching immersion, and then she lay back in blissful, relaxed exhaustion, feeling as though she had stumbled out of hell into heaven.

That sensation didn't last long, as Adam began to wash her with as much expertise as he'd shown in undressing her. His hands were reassuringly warm and gentle as he conducted an inch-by-inch examination of her injuries, but his face was anything *but* warm and gentle. His expression grew steadily more forbidding at every new bruise, scrape, or scratch he found.

When he reached for a towel and assisted her to stand upright on one foot while he dried her, Jackie felt so anxious over his deadly quiet, barely controlled inner ferocity that she involuntarily flinched as he swept her up in his arms again to carry her to the bedroom.

Adam noted her action and the wide-eyed, anxious look that accompanied it and forced his features into a slightly less intimidating mold. "I'm not angry with you," he said through stiff lips. "You can relax."

Jackie did, but only infinitesimally. His tone had not been all that convincing. "You *look* angry," she said with the first timidity she'd ever shown toward Adam. "And you sound it," she added for good measure. "What's wrong?"

Adam gave her a look that said her question was stupid, to say the least. "We'll talk about it later," he said with grim forbearance as he set her down on the bed. Then he went to the bureau and began slamming drawers open and shut with impatient ferocity as he looked for a gown for her. When he finally found one, it was a very sheer, very sexy lemon-yellow one Jackie would not have dared suggest she wear.

"This is damn skimpy," he complained gruffly, "but if you get under the covers, maybe you won't catch pneumonia. I couldn't find that warm thing you had on when we met."

Flushing a little with embarrassed remembrance that she had made sure Adam wouldn't see her in the flannel nightie again, Jackie raised her arms as he pulled the nightgown over her head, then let him settle her under the covers.

"Are you hungry?" Adam asked as he straightened up, then stood glowering down at her, hands on his hips, and with a tone in his voice that dared her to answer no to his question.

Jackie conveniently decided that she was hungry and nodded her confirmation meekly. She was afraid to say a wrong word and was feeling distinctly abused and self-pitying at Adam's harsh treatment of her.

He turned on his heels, saying he would fix her something to eat, and Jackie watched him go, blinking back tears of confused hurt. Adam was behaving as though he wouldn't have cared if she'd died out there, and after all she'd been through, his attitude was just too much! she thought. She turned her face away from the door and fought the tears with exhausted dejection until Adam returned a few moments later with a tube of antiseptic salve and a bandage. "I've got soup heating," he informed her impersonally, "but we'd better treat your cuts and wrap your ankle before you eat."

Jackie nodded, and after a few moments of Adam's ministrations, she knew it was safe to cry openly because he would attribute her tears to physical rather than emotional pain.

Adam finished, stuffed a pillow under her leg, and pulled the covers back over her. When he lifted his head and saw the tears shimmering like diamonds in Jackie's blue eyes, his expression softened and he moved to cup her cheek with a comforting hand. "I'm sorry, baby," he apologized softly. "I'll try to do better on the rest of you."

He took her hands then to apply the antiseptic, and Jackie gathered her courage to ask him about the cause of his earlier bad temper, as he seemed more his old self. "Adam?" She said his name with soft pleading in her tone. "Why have you been so angry?"

He paused in what he was doing to flash her a look from eyes suddenly more green than brown. "How would you feel if I had disappeared and then you'd found me lying hurt somewhere?" he asked with dry inquiry.

Jackie pictured it, and her eyes softened with dismay. "I'd hate it!" she said vehemently.

Adam smiled rather grimly and raised his eyebrows at her. "And I don't even have a history of trying to kill myself to join a dead spouse," he drawled with stark meaning in his tone.

Jackie stared at him in shock for a moment before she closed her eyes and swallowed down the lump in her throat. "That wasn't what I was doing, Adam," she said with quiet forcefulness. "This was an accident! I swear it!" Her eyes pleaded with him to accept the truth of her statement. "I don't want to die anymore, Adam," she added softly, gazing at him with all her love in her eyes. "Not now..."

Adam stared back at her for a long moment, and she couldn't tell from his expression whether he believed her or not. Then he applied himself to smearing the last of the antiseptic on her hands as he murmured, "You've had a bad shock. We'll talk about how it happened later." He finished, screwed the top back on the tube of antiseptic, and got to his feet. "Now it's time you ate something."

He left the room again, and Jackie collapsed against the pillows, her heart frozen with dread that Adam really believed she had been trying to kill herself again. She wished she had never told him so much about her private history. She wished he would get over his obsession with Matt. And most of all, she wished he would take her into his arms and tell her he loved her instead of looking for reasons to keep them apart.

When Adam came back, he proceeded to feed her the soup spoonful by spoonful against her weak protestations. "Adam, you don't have to feed me! I can—"

"Hush," he quieted her, placing the spoon against her lips until she opened her mouth obediently, feeling slightly bemused at receiving such tender loving care from her blatantly masculine Adam.

"Did you have dinner, Adam?" she asked solicitously when at last he removed the tray and set it on the floor.

He turned back to her and leaned across her body

while he studied her face intently. "No. I wasn't hungry," he said absently. Then, "Are you up to telling me what happened?" The change of subject was accompanied by a return to his former grimness.

Jackie stared into the depths of Adam's glinting eyes, took a deep breath, and answered, "Yes." Then she proceeded to tell him, in great detail, exactly what had happened.

When she had finished, she was relieved to see that Adam's grimness had faded. "What started the rock rolling, do you know?" he asked, his eyes narrowed in thought.

Jackie shrugged, which was a mistake, and her wincing reaction to her body's protest was immediate. "I don't know," she gasped as she eased herself into a more comfortable position. "Sometimes they just move, don't they? The ground shifts or something?" She gestured with her hand vaguely. Encouraged by Adam's softening attitude, she asked, "Tell me how you found me."

He told her then how he had returned, found her missing, and gone looking for her, in all the wrong places as it turned out, until he had finally started in the right direction, calling her from time to time. "I pictured you dead, you know!" he finished in a harsh tone, his eyes hard and cold.

"I pictured me dead a couple of times, too," Jackie joked feebly, hoping to restore his earlier softness.

She realized it was the wrong thing to say as she watched Adam's face turn to stone. "That isn't funny!" he said harshly.

Jackie drew in her breath, her eyes wide with regret, then raised a hand to stroke his cheek tenderly. "I know, darling," she apologized gently. "Believe me, I know. I told you, I don't *want* to die anymore."

Adam continued to glare at her angrily for a few seconds, but under her steady loving regard he finally relaxed. He took her hand and kissed the palm, then leaned forward to brush her lips with his. "I'd better let you get some sleep," he said with husky gruffness when he withdrew. "We'll talk more tomorrow."

Jackie couldn't protest, though she was reluctant to let him go. But she knew she was only moments away from oblivion, and she felt suddenly as though she'd been drugged and wondered if Adam had put something into the soup.

"We'll take you to the doctor tomorrow," Adam said as he moved toward the door. "I want you checked over."

"He's not there," Jackie mumbled sleepily. "I'm all right, anyway, Adam. I don't need to see him."

"You tried to see the doctor today?" Adam asked in a peculiarly strained voice that brought Jackie's drooping eyes fully open.

"Yes. I said I would," she answered on a surprised note. "I made an appointment for next week." Then her eyes flickered closed again and she murmured, "Good night, Adam," groggily.

Jackie barely heard his soft "Good night, Jack. Sleep well," and seconds later she was doing just that.

Chapter Ten

For Jackie the next two days were a mixture of physical torture and emotional upheaval, while at the same time, from a purely intellectual standpoint, they were extremely interesting. She watched and felt herself falling more and more irrevocably in love with Adam, almost as though she had a separate facility in her brain to be used for cataloging what was happening to her on another level.

Adam was that rare and fascinating combination sometimes found among the male species—and always to be treasured when it was—of total masculinity coupled with tender, humorous gentleness that almost made it a pleasure to be sick when he was doing the caretaking. She exaggerated her woes, complained loudly over minor inconveniences, and made a thorough nuisance of herself for no other reason than to see Adam's reaction.

She felt oddly discouraged when he passed every test with flying colors. Did he suspect what she was doing? she asked herself with wary suspicion. But how could he? And why would he go along with her if he did? No, she decided glumly, he must just be as perfect as he seemed, and since he was, why would he want to get involved with a bad-tempered, sarcastic, accident-prone nitwit like her?

By the evening of the second day she was sunk in gloomy contemplation of her various inadequacies when compared with Adam's attributes. The balance sheet was so skewn, it seemed beyond straightening. Broodingly she watched him where he sat in the only armchair the cabin possessed, cleaning his rifle, while she lay on the couch with her ankle propped up.

"I'm sorry I've spoiled your hunting the last couple of days, Adam." She made a bid for his attention with what she thought was admirable restraint. "You must be eager to get back to it." This was another test, and she listened with increasing gloom as he passed it, too.

"Not at all," he answered pleasantly. "I'm glad I'm here to look after you. You'd have been in real trouble had you been staying here by yourself."

Jackie sighed in discouraged agreement, feeling an unaccountable rise of irritation at Adam's kindness. Darn him! Didn't he have *any* faults? It was like being in love with a saint!

"After I've seen the doctor and buy a cane to get around with, you can probably resume your hunting," she said on almost a sulky note. She had explained to Adam that since she had already made an appointment for Tuesday morning, and since her ankle wasn't broken, it made sense to wait and have him check her over at her scheduled appointment. Adam had eventually agreed, but without a word of acknowledgment that he knew why she had made the original appointment.

"No hurry," Adam answered her with casual unconcern. "I have plenty of time." And he continued cleaning his rifle with no indication that he'd heard the sulky note in her voice. Jackie felt like throwing something at him. His manner since the accident had been full of concern, but he hadn't displayed even a tinge of the romantic interest she craved from him.

By now, on a purely superficial level, they were as intimately acquainted as any husband and wife except physically, but while Jackie reveled in every casual touch he gave her, Adam seemed as unmoved as a stone.

"You're so kind," she said on a sour note of insincerity.

Adam looked up, his eyes glinting dangerously and his mouth tugged into a smile of amused masculine tolerance. "Am I?" he said with easy dryness. "Perhaps I deserve a medal for it if I am, considering you've been trying to goad me into being anything *but* kind for the last two days."

Jackie adopted a look of cool surprise, while inwardly she felt a twinge of uneasy alarm. "I don't know what you're talking about," she said with a sniff in her voice. "I may have been a little out of sorts," she graciously admitted. "I *am* in a great deal of pain, you know." She tried to sound pitiful, but the look of mocking awareness in Adam's eyes warned her that she'd better stress the pity angle a little stronger. Adam seemed to be in a dangerous mood for some reason, and somehow, she didn't think it was a good time to provoke him unduly. "I wouldn't deliberately *goad* you, Adam," she said with wide-eyed innocence. "It's just that I find physical pain so hard to bear." There, she thought with canny satisfaction. She had projected just the right note of brave endurance in the face of tremendous odds.

Adam set aside his rifle with casual indifference, stretched his legs out toward the fire, and rested his head against the back of the chair. "Come on, Jack," he drawled lazily. "Admit it. You've been testing me, ordering me to do this, complaining about that— you've been having a ball." He cocked an inquisitive eyebrow at her, but the note of danger was still strong in his voice. "What I want to know is, *why*?"

Jackie shifted uncomfortably under his knowing eyes, wincing as the movement disturbed her ankle. "Really, Adam," she scoffed uneasily. "You have quite an imagination. "I haven't—"

"Yes, my sweet, you have," he interrupted her, and suddenly he was leaning forward and grinning engagingly. "Now, be a good girl and tell me why."

Jackie sulked. She wasn't about to tell Adam she had been in the process of falling more in love with him and had used her bitchiness in an attempt to find a defense against that love.

After a moment of silence when she didn't answer him, Adam got to his feet and came to sit beside her on the couch, ignoring her alarmed protests, admonitions to be careful of her ankle, and general anxiousness. He had her imprisoned and he reached one hand to play with the tie of her negligee with tantalizing negligence. "Did you want to see how much I would take?" he murmured with teasing huskiness. "Did you want to see how far you could push before I began to push back?"

Jackie bit her lip and looked at him cautiously from beneath her lashes, giving an unconvincing shake of her head. Her hair was down, lying in luxuriant waves on her shoulders, and Adam took a handful of it and tugged playfully. "I warn you, Jack," he said with dangerous softness. "I'm about ready to push back if you don't come clean."

His hair tugging was causing delicious thrills to emanate from her scalp downward, and she could feel the warmth of his body reaching out to her in mesmerizing waves. Finally, she lifted drowsy passion-clouded eyes to his and pleaded silently for reprieve. Adam answered the plea with a soft teasing kiss on her parted lips. "Why, Jack?" he murmured against her mouth, and then she felt his tongue tracing the outline of her lips with devastating effect.

She wished he wouldn't talk anymore so that he could concentrate on kissing her. It was the first time in days that he had shown her any sexual interest, and she was reacting like a starving kitten presented with a saucer of milk. All she wanted was to feel. She didn't want to think, and she especially didn't want to parry Adam's questions. She raised her mouth to try to capture Adam's, but he moved back just out of reach. "Answer me," he demanded with soft inflexibility.

Jackie sighed with frustration and relaxed back against the pillow supporting her. It was obvious Adam wasn't going to give her what she wanted until she gave *him* what he demanded. "That's blackmail," she muttered revealingly, unaware for a moment that her remark told him just how badly she needed his lovemaking. When she saw the wicked glint of knowing amusement in his eyes, she realized the implications of what she'd said and she flushed in discomfort at her stupidity, thinking it was despicable of Adam to show feet of clay at last at *her* expense. No gentleman would have shown so clearly that he understood and was amused by her physical needs.

Perversely, she decided that since she'd already shown him that much, she might as well jump in with both feet and hope they didn't end up in her mouth, as well. "I wanted to see if you were as perfect as you seemed," she admitted with all the cross sulkiness of a poor loser, which normally she was not. "You were such a paragon, I couldn't believe it. It was disgusting!"

Adam stared at her in disbelief for a moment, then threw back his head and whooped with laughter. Jackie watched with growing rebelliousness, but in the end his enjoyment was so infectious, her mouth began twitching with amusement, too. When Adam finally controlled his mirth and looked down at her with blatant admiration in his eyes, she was openly grinning.

"You're something else," he told her, shaking his head in incredulity. "A man could live with you for fifty years and never grow bored. He'd never know from one moment to the next what you'd come up with to amuse, exasperate, or tantalize him with!"

Jackie's heart seemed to stop in midbeat at his words. Was that an idle compliment or something more? she wondered. "That's what Matt always said," she answered thoughtlessly, and then could have bitten her tongue out when she saw the amusement in Adam's eyes die.

"I'll bet he did," he said musingly. "And he must have been cut from the same cloth as you, since you miss him so terribly."

Jackie couldn't decide if what she heard in his voice was really regretful sadness or if she was imagining things. With pounding pulses she wondered if he was feeling sad for her or for himself. She searched for a way to reassure him in case it was the later. "I did, yes," she said with husky meaningfulness. "I always will, in a way. But lately I've come to accept that he's gone. I don't hurt anymore."

Adam gave her a sharp glance, searching her face with a penetrating scrutiny that she bore with her heart in her eyes. Slowly his look changed to one of aching hunger, and as he bent his head to hers, Jackie closed her eyes in a helpless drowning of emotion. She met his kiss with a moan from deep in her throat that seemed to release a savage intensity in Adam. His kiss went quickly from tentative searching to deep, demanding forcefulness, and Jackie felt the tensions and worries of the last few moments uncurl inside her into a flooding heat of exultant desire to give and take, please and be pleased.

Adam seemed starving for the taste of her, his mouth sliding from hers to caress her cheek, nibble the lobe of her ear, and search out the throbbing pulse of her throat with lips and tongue. He pushed aside her thin negligee and gathered the fullness of her breast into his hand to lift it to his mouth and tease the nipple with expert sensitivity until Jackie was gasping with pleasure, uttering incoherent pleas for Adam's ultimate possession.

She could feel the sexual tension in him, the striving for release that made his skin hot to the touch, his breathing harsh, and his body shudder with the longing to take her irrevocably.

"Adam, please," Jackie begged, stroking the dark head at her breast and writhing with pleasure at the sensations evoked by his roaming hands and mouth. "Love me, Adam," she pleaded with aching need. "Please, love me!"

Adam raised his head and Jackie inhaled sharply at the look of blazing passion and determination he gave her. "I'm going to," he promised in a ragged tone that was nevertheless forceful enough to convince her he meant what he said. "I'm going to make you mine once and for all, and then I'm going to take you home and marry you and keep you safe!"

Jackie's eyes widened with astonishment at his declaration, then shone with joy as she took in the implications of the commitment he was making. "Yes— oh, yes, Adam!" she breathed her response on a soft sigh of happiness. "I love you so much."

"You'd better," he said as though making a vow, his eyes holding her own with purposefulness. "Because I love you, and I'm going to seal that love right now. You aren't going to get the chance for second thoughts."

"I don't need any second thoughts, Adam," Jackie vowed in her own turn, putting all the love and sincerity she felt in her tone. "I know what I want."

Adam held her gaze for a long moment, then kissed her with hard urgency before pulling away to get to his feet and lift her into his arms. He started toward the bedroom while Jackie clung to his neck, her heart speeding up into a frantic rhythm of anticipation, her lips soft against his cheek and ear, her tremulous breath telling him of her need.

He set her gently down on the bed, then straightened to begin undoing his shirt, his eyes holding hers all the while. Jackie gazed up at him, reveling in the complete maleness of his look, feeling as though she might burst with happiness at any moment. "When did you decide, Adam?" she asked softly as she avidly watched him fling away his shirt and start to undo his jeans after first reaching into his pocket to extract something she couldn't see in the dim light.

"The morning of the day you got hurt," he said, his voice rasping with his impatience to come to her. He stepped out of the rest of his clothing, revealing himself to her eyes with stunning unselfconsciousness of his own beauty, then bent to grapple with the tie of her negligee with impatient hands. "What you said got through to me," he murmured almost absently as the negligee fell away, and he feasted his eyes on the smooth skin of her shoulders and the tops of her swelling breasts above her nightgown. Jackie wriggled out of the nightgown, as impatient as he was to have no further barriers between them, and Adam came down to her to stretch himself full length over her, his gaze hotly wanting as he held her own. "I decided I didn't care whether I was as wise as Solomon," he said thickly, tracing her mouth with his own. "Wisdom can't hold a candle to loving."

"Oh, Adam..." Jackie gasped as he shifted his

weight to place the heat of his need against hers. "I'm so glad. You've been so distant, I was afraid you didn't want me anymore."

He gave an unamused laugh. "You can feel I do, can't you?" he whispered against her neck, his voice unsteady.

"Yes...now..." Jackie murmured, arching toward him, running her hands over his smooth, tautly muscled back. "But in the past few days—"

"You were hurt," he explained huskily. "And I needed time to believe you really were over Matt— that you weren't lying to yourself and to me about the accident."

"I wasn't, Adam," Jackie murmured, cupping his head in her hands to show him with her eyes that she meant what she said.

"I believe you," he affirmed, returning her loving gaze. "But even if I didn't, I'd make love to you anyway. When I was afraid you were lost to me, I realized I don't want to spend the rest of my life without you. I love you enough to satisfy both of us."

"I'll help you with the loving," Jackie promised solemnly, her lips curving into an invitation that darkened Adam's eyes into a sensuous warmth. She felt him give an involuntary thrust toward her with his manhood, and it was only then that she remembered this loving could result in a child. Her eyes widened with the knowledge, and she drew back slightly to fix him with an anxious gaze. "Adam, I'm still not protected," she said hesitantly, hating to remind him but unwilling to have him blame himself if she should become pregnant.

"Don't worry," he whispered with a wicked grin. "I'm going to take care of that. When I realized I was too far over the brink to come back, I followed you into town to make sure I didn't have to spend any more cold nights on the floor. I wasn't sure you could get in to see the doctor, or even if you still wanted to after our fight. I wasn't taking any chances."

"Oh, Adam..." Jackie breathed her delight with his admission, though she didn't tell him she'd seen him in town that day, nor what she'd thought when she had seen him. "It doesn't really matter, you know," she confessed softly against his mouth. "I want children as much as you do."

"Yes, but not just yet," Adam growled, wrapping her more closely against him. "I want my wife to myself for a little while. A child can come along after I've had enough of you not to mind sharing you with someone else."

Jackie opened her mouth to express her whole-hearted concurrence with his wishes, but Adam closed it with a kiss. "Shhh..." he said huskily against her lips. "We've talked enough. Let's communicate another way."

With an eager nod Jackie opened her mouth under his to his kiss, then opened her body to him with even more eagerness, submitting to his urgent hunger with her own, unfolding to his possession with every nuance of love and passion in her, until they both stepped over the brink into commitment to each other forever.

Chapter Eleven

Jackie's dream was deliciously intoxicating. Adam was making love to her, and it seemed so real, she could actually *feel* his warm palms stroking her bare flesh, his mouth tantalizing the flesh on her nape, his hard length curved around and pressing into her back and thighs and calves without an inch of space between them anywhere. Even his toes were in contact with hers, rubbing and teasing and provoking her into hoping she would never wake up from this particular dream.

Gradually, however, as Adam's lovemaking grew more urgent and his explorations more intimate, consciousness began leaking through in reluctant little dribs and drabs that finally brought Jackie's eyes blinking sluggishly open and her senses to an awareness that no dream could possibly be *this* real.

"Turn over, Jack." She heard Adam's soft slurred morning voice in her ear even as his hands were putting his direction into effect.

When they were face to face, Jackie didn't have time to question or to wonder, even had she wanted to, for Adam's mouth covered hers immediately, sipping delicately at first until Jackie's lips parted to allow entrance to his gently probing tongue. She shuddered at the invasion that followed, noting in her half-asleep, bemused sensitivity that there was something different about Adam's approach this morning— something more purposeful and determined and inevitable than she had sensed from him before.

"Jack . . . touch me," he crooned softly against her mouth, catching her hand where it lay lightly clasped on his shoulder and drawing it down his side to his thigh, then bringing it back up again, establishing a motion that she blindly followed when he let go of her hand. It seemed entirely natural that Adam was nude, as was she, and that they were in bed together, waking up together, making love together, as though they did this every morning.

For long, sleepy, yet strangely aware moments they caressed each other with unhurried enjoyment, letting their hands and mouths stroke and taste and explore in silence except for gentle sighs and barely murmured endearments. But then Adam stepped the pace up by slow degrees, seeming to sense with exquisite accuracy that any sudden escalation of his part might break the somnambulant bubble of natural response where Jackie dwelled.

Once again he took her hand, bringing it lower than his waist, yet just short of his desire. It was close enough, however, that both of them felt a sudden breathlessness that presaged a stronger, more driving need in their separate entities to strive for an abnegation of that separateness.

"Adam..." His name came from low in her throat and was spoken with a sighing acceptance that was all Adam needed to launch a stronger offensive on their mutual desire. Jackie felt his muscles tauten under her hands, felt his mouth widen over hers and take possession with more power, more dominance than he had previously shown. She reveled in his ever increasing need to take from her every nuance of erotic desire he fostered, then plundered.

Now he was over her, positioning her for satisfaction of the needs he had created, and his half-hooded, desire-laden eyes glittered into hers as he held her gaze with total compulsion, his mouth twisted into a dominating half-smile.

"I'm going to love you," he promised in a grating, almost harsh, though very soft tone.

And even as Jackie was breathing "Yes..." in a drawn-out half-sobbing whisper, he entered the sanctuary of her body with a convulsive thrust that seemed uncontrollable, yet was exquisitely controlled.

Jackie's immersion in Adam was so complete, she felt as though she were drowning in him, merging with him totally, losing her individuality in a more satisfying joining than was possible in lonely selfhood. Without conscious effort she flowed into his rhythm as though she had always known it, as if it were implanted in her tissues and bones indelibly and had been for infinity.

The rhythm increased, spiraled out of control, exploded into star bursts of agonizing pleasure, leaving them both gasping, shuddering, holding on to one another for balance in a world gone suddenly out of orbit. And then gradually, slowly, deliciously, reality settled around them again, and they lay exhausted in one another's arms, their mutual contentment casting an aura of loving complicity that was almost tangible in its force.

Jackie was in no hurry to disturb that aura. She felt boneless, yet exhilarated; tired, yet filled with a bubbling energy that came from the feel of her beautiful Adam stretched on top of her in languorous relaxation, his powerful form a welcome pressure she savored tenderly as she stroked his shoulders in a gentling massage that continued down his back before circling his waist in a firm embrace. She murmured unintelligibly against his thick hair, not knowing or caring what she said, merely wanting to express in tone her depthless love for him.

Finally, reluctantly, Adam raised himself, took Jackie's face into his palms, and subjected her to an intense scrutiny that could only have shown him what her heart was saying inaudibly. At seeing a satisfactory aftermath to what he had precipitated, he smiled, a slow, contented, sleepy, loving smile.

"That was lesson number two in how to start the day right," he murmured with gentle mockery. "Good morning, Jack."

"Good morning, Adam." She smiled back, her face flushed and sweet-looking in its softness. "Do I get an A for having passed your test?"

He considered for a second, then nodded his head, a glint of mischievousness in his eyes. "I think A plus would be more appropriate. You certainly have a knack for learning, and I can't fault your enthusiasm."

"Thank you," Jackie replied demurely. "But I can't take false credit. The instructor—and the subject—make all the difference in the world to how fast and how enthusiastically I learn a lesson."

They were smiling at each other with perfect understanding and contentment when a loud knocking on the front door startled both of them into identical expressions of shocked incredulity. Neither could imagine who, for the first time since they'd shared the cabin, could be violating their privacy.

Adam recovered first. "Stay where you are," he ordered Jackie as he moved to climb out of bed. "I'll get rid of whoever it is, and then we have some things to discuss."

The intrusion of the outside world into their sanctuary, plus Adam's statement that they were going to talk, brought Jackie out of her dreamworld in a hurry. Her eyes were wide and anxious as she watched Adam get up, and then they softened with pleasure as she studied his beautiful physique and remembered it was all hers.

"Hurry back," she admonished him in a teasing voice and was delighted when his words echoed his roguish grin.

"Try to keep me away," he teased back as he fastened his jeans, then strode toward the door. "Don't get up," he commanded softly as he left, causing Jackie to lie back against the pillows in accordance with his wishes.

A moment later, however, she sat up, startled at hearing John Reardon's voice in the living room. Wondering what in the world their mutual landlord

could want, she decided that despite Adam's telling
her to stay where she was, a little eavesdropping
might be prudent and that the addition of at least a
robe to her naked body might be even more so should
Mr. Reardon's visit stretch out.

When she got to the bedroom door, pulling on her
robe as she went, she heard Adam and Mr. Reardon
exchanging conventional greetings, and she winced a
little at hearing the landlord's rather strained tone,
thinking he must be uncomfortable at disturbing
them at this early hour, though she thought his discomfort must be even more acute at knowing they
weren't married.

Then she grew still as she heard Mr. Reardon in-
forming Adam that he had had a telephone call from a
Miss Bowie in Montana and had been requested to
relay the message that she wanted him to call back
immediately.

"Did she say it was an emergency?" Adam asked
in a thoughtful, almost irritated tone.

"Nope," the landlord replied with western brevity.
"But I figured it was, since she insisted I come all the
way up here to tell you to call back pronto."

After a pause, Adam answered the tone in Mr.
Reardon's voice that said he had been severely incon-
venienced. "I'm sorry about that, John," he apologized. "It was good of you to go to the trouble."

"Well..." Mr. Reardon sounded mollified somewhat, and though Jackie couldn't see it, his eyes were
roaming the interior of the cabin with a great deal of
curiosity. But Adam could see it, and he was well
aware of the reason for John Reardon's scrutiny.

"I'd offer you a cup of coffee, John," he said with the barest trace of cynicism, "but as you can see, I've just gotten up, and there's none made. Besides, I wouldn't want to keep you from your work any longer than necessary, especially when I've already been the cause of your having to take time off to come all the way up here."

"Well..." John Reardon said again, reluctance to leave in his tone. It was obvious he was wondering where Jackie was, as his eyes kept darting toward the closed bedroom door, but Adam started moving the man toward the front door, his expression polite but firm.

"Thank you again, John," Adam said as he opened the door to the outside world and waited with barely suppressed impatience for the man to leave. "Tell Mrs. Reardon hello for me."

Jackie barely heard John Reardon's reluctant good-bye or Adam's more cheerful one. She was anxious to learn if the landlord's message meant she and Adam were going to have to leave earlier than she had thought, because of some emergency at his office back in Montana. And as much as she wanted to start her new life with Adam, she found herself reluctant to leave the sanctuary they had found here together.

Barely had the front door closed behind Mr. Reardon before she opened the bedroom door and stepped through to see Adam standing in deep thought. "Is Miss Bowie your secretary?" she asked anxiously, coming up to Adam to wrap her arms around his waist. Then she wished she hadn't asked when she saw a careful look come into his hazel eyes.

"No," he said quietly, moving to place his arms around her and studying her suddenly arrested expression with interest. "She's the woman I came up here to think about marrying."

"Oh." Jackie said the one word in a small voice, but her stiffened posture spelled out her jealousy. "Then I guess you'd better get dressed and go find out what she wants," she added with a careful lack of emphasis.

At that Adam's look changed to one of tender amusement, and he dropped a kiss onto the top of Jackie's downcast head. "I'll call her later, sweetheart," he said gravely. "If there is an emergency, I can't imagine what I can do about it from here. There are people closer to home she can call on if she needs help."

Jackie eyed him uncertainly, mollified by his refusal to rush to return the call, but still unhappy at having the woman in Montana intrude into their lives on this, of all mornings. "I'm going to make some coffee."

Adam reached a hand to her shoulder to stop her. "Then come back and join me in the bedroom. You weren't supposed to leave it in the first place, remember?"

Jackie eyed him a little mutinously, but responding to the teasing note in his voice, she moved to do as he asked while he entered the bathroom. She heard him walk out again just as she was putting the coffee on the stove, and saw him disappear into the bedroom as she went to use the bathroom herself. A few moments later she went to the bedroom to find him stretched out in the bed, looking for all the world like a king awaiting his concubine and his morning coffee.

She scowled in response to his cheerful smile and offered him the cup of coffee she'd brought him while she sat on the side of the bed and began to sip her own.

"If I didn't know better," Adam said after taking a hearty drink of his coffee, "I'd say you were jealous. But of course you're not, are you?" he asked innocently.

Jackie glared at him, then settled her features into a sweet look. "Who, me?" She batted her eyes at him in mock astonishment. "Now, why would I be jealous simply because a woman you've been thinking about marrying calls you and interrupts our first morning in bed together?"

Adam's reaction was maddeningly calm. "But I'm not thinking about marrying her anymore, am I?" he asked reasonably. "I haven't been for some time. I'm going to marry a bad-tempered, hot-blooded widow."

Mollified by his reaffirmation of his proposal of the night before, Jackie nevertheless fixed him with a petulant eye. "Then why is she calling you?" she asked illogically.

Adam shrugged. "She's probably wondering why I haven't called her since I've been here. I promised to, but somehow it...er...slipped my mind."

Jackie stared at him, then melted at the teasing, warming look of love in his eyes. "I could maybe make it slip your mind again," she offered in a small voice of apology.

"You can make *anything* slip my mind," Adam responded gratifyingly as he set his cup aside. "Come here and I'll show you."

Jackie slid into his waiting arms eagerly, her mouth urgent with the need to claim him as her own again. Adam tugged the robe from her shoulders and drew her beneath the covers with him, but when he had her helpless beneath him, he held back.

"I didn't actually ask you if you'd marry me, did I?" he murmured endearingly. "I told you you were going to. Maybe we'd better start off right. Will you marry me, Jackie?"

Jackie couldn't resist tantalizing him, though her eyes were soft with her real answer. "Maybe..." she prevaricated. "It depends on—"

But Adam sighed and shook his head in disgust. "I have to teach you everything," he complained. "Now listen carefully, sweetheart. When a man proposes to a woman, she can say yes, or she can say no. That's all that is required." He hesitated, then fixed her with a purposeful look. "Unless the man had decided he won't take no for an answer."

Jackie started giggling, and Adam lowered his head to nibble her lower lip, which stopped her laughter on a gasp, and then between stroking her trembling mouth with his tongue, he husked, "It's against my principles to make love to an uncommitted woman. Say yes, Jack, and say it fast."

"Ha!" she managed. "It didn't stop you last night or this morning."

"I have lapses in my principles," he explained patiently. "Especially where you're concerned. Aren't you going to say yes?"

"I don't know yet," she teased, and then ended on a groan as Adam found her breast to tease and fondle.

"Say it, Jack."

Jackie's eyes fluttered open to revel in the love she saw gleaming back at her in Adam's. "Yes," she said softly. "I'lf marry you, Adam Clarke. A judge shouldn't have lapses in principle, and someone needs to keep you on the straight and narrow."

"Is that the only reason?" Adam persisted on a soft chuckle.

"Well, I love you a little bit, too," Jackie responded tenderly.

A faint hurt appeared in Adam's eyes as he asked, "About one-third as much as—"

"No, Adam!" Jackie hastily reassured him. "One whole. I love you with *all* my heart! Please believe that!"

There was such sincerity in her tone that Adam relaxed and murmured, "I do." And then more strongly, "Oh, God, yes, I do! And I love you with all of me." He buried his mouth in her arched throat and growled, "I want to give and give and give..." His voice died away as he slid lower to begin his magnanimous generosity.

"And I want to take and take and take..." Jackie groaned, twisting under his marauding, possessive mouth and hands.

"Then do it" was Adam's last coherent statement before he began to give her all he had, and Jackie responded by giving as much as she took, until both of them were sated with both sides of the loving coin.

Chapter Twelve

"You certainly are bossy!" Jackie grumbled happily as she untangled herself from the strewn bedclothes sometime later, preparing to get up and begin to put into effect the very succinct, very adamant plans for her future Adam had just finished outlining.

"If I am, it's because I have a feeling I'd better start this relationship off on the offensive before I lose any hope of controlling you at all," Adam responded with tart dryness.

Jackie hooted as she got to her feet and gave a long stretch of absolute contentment with the various little sorenesses that were an aftermath of Adam's loving. "If you ask me, you're too used to having your own way all the time, Judge. A man needs a little contention in his life to keep from becoming absolutely unbearable."

"Something tells me I'm not going to have to worry about that possibility from here on out," Adam retorted, though there was a smile in his tone, and if Jackie had looked at him at that moment, she would have seen such relishment of the prospect in Adam's dancing eyes, she would have been even happier than she already was. But she didn't, and when she turned around to look at Adam, his expression was smoothed into blandness.

"Adam..." she said hesitantly, her eyes wide and serious, her tone suddenly sober. "I'll *try* to control my temper, if it really bothers you, but—"

Adam could barely keep a straight face while viewing Jackie's obvious dilemma. She looked like a small child with her tousled hair, her huge blue eyes, biting her lip and twisting her hands, exactly as though she'd been caught being naughty and wanted to be good, but was not, in all honesty, certain she could live up to any elaborate promises.

"I wouldn't worry about it too much," he said soberly. "I think I can take care of myself in the temper department."

Jackie blinked at him for a moment, then a smile started tugging at the corners of her sweet mouth. "Yes..." she said slowly, then burst into a spontaneous giggle. "I think you can, Adam Clarke. And it's a good thing, too. I'd hate to have to go around feeling guilty for the rest of my life for browbeating a grown man."

Adam's growl made her laughter peal out, and she ducked back out of the way of his reaching hand. "Come on, Adam," she protested. "If we're going to put your timetable into effect, we've got things to do. Get up from there and get busy, you lazy lecherous man!"

A few hours later, after everything that was theirs had been stowed in Adam's pickup, and Jackie's car had been affixed with a towline to the back of it, she paused for one last look at the mountain cabin that had been the site responsible for coloring her future days with joy rather than with loneliness. Tears misted her eyes, and she felt a strong reluctance to give up this sanctuary from the rest of humanity and to go back into a world where she would have to share Adam.

Adam came to her side and wrapped his arms around her, studying the look in her eyes. "If you'd rather stay here longer, we can unpack everything again," he said sympathetically. "It's just that I wanted to get you home and marry you while I still have time for us to have a honeymoon. My calendar is so full once I get back to work, we won't have a chance to spend as much time together alone as I want after I've put that ring on your finger."

Jackie smiled tremulously up at him and shook her head. "It's all right," she answered, her pleasure in his thoughtfulness evident in her tone. "I would like to come back someday, though," she half-questioned.

"Don't worry," he replied softly, "I'm not going to overlook any opportunity to have you completely to myself, and even if this place didn't have special significance for us, its isolation fills the bill admirably. We'll be back next year."

"Promise?" Jackie teased, delighted with his possessiveness.

"Promise," he answered soberly, his eyes drowning her with love.

Jackie studied the inherent integrity in Adam's rugged face and heard the tone in his voice that told her she could believe his promises, and she wrapped her arms around him to rest for a moment against the solid bulk of his strong body. "I believe you, Adam," she murmured happily. "I'll always believe you."

"You can, Jack," he responded huskily. "I take care of my own."

A thrill of belonging raced her spine for an instant before she stepped back and wiped her eyes. "Okay, then," she said firmly. "Let's go to Montana."

They stopped by the Reardons to drop off the keys and what perishables they had left and so that Adam could say good-bye to them. Jackie wasn't sure she wanted to face Mrs. Reardon again, but Adam teased her into it. "You don't want her to think you're just a one-month stand, do you?" he said laughingly as he pulled her out of the car. "We've got to repair your reputation, or they might not let us come back."

Still, Jackie thought a few moments later as she noted the coolness in Mrs. Reardon's beady little eyes, she could have done without being viewed as a latter-day jezebel even for the sake of future occupancy of the cabin. But Adam, as usual, was irresistible, and before the two of them got on their way again, Mrs. Reardon had warmed up considerably, especially upon learning that Adam and Jackie were to be married before another week had gone by.

"Whew!" Jackie breathed a sigh of relief when they were back in the pickup. "You have my whole-hearted respect, Adam. Anyone who can charm that dragon belongs in a diplomatic corp, not on a judge's seat."

Adam laughed. "It's obvious you don't know much

about what goes on in a courtroom, then. Even Solomon would have his hands full these days."

Jackie gave him a look full of prideful love. "That's one thing I'm looking forward to, darling. I can't wait to see you all decked out in black robes, banging your gavel, and dispensing wisdom right and left. It gives me goosebumps to think about."

"Good God, woman!" Adam shot her a look of alarm. "Do you mean I'm about to marry a judicial groupie?"

Jackie smiled at him with sweet innocence. "Revelation number one about your intended. Isn't it going to be fun finding out all these little quirks in our characters?" Then her smile slipped into a stern frown. "But just remember, when you get home at night, the robes come off, the gavel gets put away, and the wisdom is to be shared *very* tactfully."

Adam chuckled, then reached over to draw her closer to his side. He took his eyes off the road for a moment to gaze down at her with lustful love. "I'll remember that, little spitfire, if you'll remember that groupies are generally willing to do *anything* for the object of their adoration."

"Hmmm," Jackie parried, cuddling against him contentedly. "As a writer, I'm very conscious of the meaning of words. Let's define *anything*."

"Let's wait until I can stop driving and get my hands on you properly," Adam countered. "Definitions are usually made clearer with demonstrations."

Despite the bone-shaking ride in Adam's pickup, the scenery was so entrancing that Jackie managed to overlook her aching body's protests most of the time.

At seeing an antelope grazing side by side with cattle in a pasture, however, she remembered with some puzzlement that Adam hadn't brought back even one deer to show for his hunting trip, and she asked him about it.

A sly grin tugged at his mouth as he glanced down at her puzzled features. "You didn't think I was going to drag back one of those brown-eyed, beautiful creatures and test your newfound understanding of the sport when I was trying to win you?" he asked teasingly. "I may be a lot of things, but stupid isn't one of them."

"Oh, Adam." Jackie beamed at him, reaching up to give him a loving peck on the cheek. "That's sweet. You really are a darling, aren't you?"

"Yep," he agreed immodestly. "Smart, too."

"But what did you do all day if you didn't shoot at anything?" she asked him.

He shrugged. "I told you I love this country and that I like the tramping about as much as anything." He slanted down a smugly teasing look at her then and added, "But the next time we come here we'll be married, and the moratorium will be lifted. You're going to love venison stew."

"Adam!" Jackie frowned at him ferociously, her tone threatening.

"Jackie!" he mocked her laughingly. "You can have my heart—in fact, you already do—but you can't have *everything*! A man's got to draw a line somewhere."

Jackie disagreed, but she didn't pursue the matter further, even though she was sure, despite her intel-

lectual understanding of hunting, that she and her
new husband were going to have one monumental
fight the first time he dragged home the corpse of
such a beautiful species.

As they neared Missoula, Jackie began to experience certain misgivings about her reception, since
they planned to stay with Adam's sister for the few
days left until his house was refurbished and ready for
occupancy. She didn't know how Adam's sibling was
going to take the idea of Adam marrying someone
whose history was perilously synonymous with her
own.

Jackie shifted nervously, disturbing the box at her
feet, in which her manuscript rested. She had been
unwilling to let it out of her sight in case Adam discovered it and started reading it before she got it finished. She had some revisions to make in the very
personal story before she would feel able to let Adam
read the words where he figured so prominently.

"What's that?" Adam asked curiously, eyeing the
box.

Jackie shot him a nervous look, but her tone was
calm when she answered. "Oh, just an...er...wed-
ding present for you. You can't see it now," she added
hastily when Adam's astonishment turned to eager
anticipation. "I've some work to do on it first."

"But what is it?" Adam persisted, his eyes narrow-
ing suspiciously. "And how could you have a wedding
present already? My God, we just decided to get married this morning!"

Jackie sniffed. "Some presents are all-occasion
gifts," she said mysteriously, and then "Watch the

road!'' as the pickup wavered uncertainly. But Adam didn't pursue the subject, for which Jackie was exceedingly grateful, and before long he was pulling up in front of a lovely home on the outskirts of Missoula.

"Adam, I'm a little scared," Jackie said in a low childlike voice. "What if your sister doesn't like me? What if—"

She had been about to ask what would happen if his sister tried to talk Adam out of marrying her, but Adam brushed her fears aside. "Nobody could possibly not like you," he asserted positively, pleasing her with his certainty if not his logic. "Now, come on. The best way to dispose of fear is to meet the object of it head on."

As it turned out there was no time for Jackie's fears to build. Adam's sister, Helena, accompanied by a small dynamo complete with towhead and mischievous smile, came out of the house to greet them. Helena was a darker haired, smaller version of Adam, and Jackie liked her on sight. She was more than pleased when the feeling appeared to be mutual. Helena's smile couldn't have been more welcoming, and the first words out of her lovely mouth might have been designed to put Jackie's fears to rest.

"When Adam called and said he was bringing me home a future sister-in-law, I was pleased, but disbelieving. I didn't think any woman could bring this confirmed bachelor to heel. But seeing you, I believe it, and I couldn't be happier." And then she hugged and kissed Jackie with such sincerity that Jackie couldn't sustain a single doubt in the face of Helena's warmth. She did wonder, however, if Helena was friends with the woman Adam had been thinking of marrying before, and she wondered furthermore just when Adam was going to return that woman's call, but now was not the time to ask either question.

"Come meet your new aunt, Marc," Helena called to her son, who was hanging on the running board of the pickup, inspecting its interior with fascination.

The little blond boy climbed down reluctantly and grinned when Adam tousled his hair. Then he approached Jackie and gazed up at her with intent inspection. He was such a darling that Jackie's heart constricted at the thought of having a boy just like him—and in the very near future, if Adam's views on the subject held sway. Since they were identical to her own, she was certain they would.

"Hi, Marc," she said happily. "Want a stick of gum?"

Warming rapidly to a woman who had the good sense to attach herself to his adored uncle and carry gum to share to boot, Marc accepted the offering, held it in one small grubby hand for a second, then smiled beatifically and gestured Jackie down to his level. She stooped to his level and matched him look for look. "I like you better than Miss Bowie," he whispered in her ear, thereby winning himself a place in Jackie's heart that was set in cement for all time.

"Good," she whispered back. "Adam does, too. I'm glad you take after him, don't you?"

He nodded solemnly, then gravely took her hand to escort her into his house and his family with all the instant acceptance of the innocent.

Helena showed Jackie to her room, and at realizing

she and Adam were going to have to sleep apart until the wedding, Jackie shot him a look of regret that he echoed with a grin, though his own eyes were regretful, as well. Then, as it was late afternoon, Helena offered to fix a meal, and Jackie trailed her into the kitchen to help while Adam played with Marc.

Helena and Jackie's rapport was so immediate that Jackie hesitated to introduce a painful subject, but midway through the meal preparations she turned to her future sister-in-law and said with all the sincerity she could command, "Helena, I'll make him happy. I promise you I will."

Helena looked startled, then her hazel eyes, which were so like Adam's, saddened a little. "I know you will, Jackie. Adam's not a fool like I was. He always knows what he's doing."

Jackie came to put her arm around Helena. "He told me about your second marriage, Helena...as a warning to me, because he thought I might be doing the same thing you did. I'm sorry things didn't work out for you."

Helena shrugged and smiled. "I am, too," she said softly, regret in her tone. But then she straightened and looked at Jackie more purposefully. "But seeing you and Adam together makes me realize that happiness is possible the second time around, or in my case, the third." She chuckled at Jackie's wide-eyed look. "I met someone while Adam was away, Jackie," she confessed half-sheepishly. "I'm not sure yet, but I think..." She shrugged again, but this time a burden seemed to be lifted from her shoulders. "Anyway, I'm going to take my time, and I'm going to be a lot more willing to at least try than I've been in the past.''

"Good for you!" Jackie praised sincerely, her blue eyes shining happily. "I know it's hard, but I can promise you it's worth it!"

"Yes, I can see you think so," Helena replied gravely, her eyes twinkling with amusement. "Now, let's get dinner over with, so we can make some plans. I'm as excited about this wedding as if it were my own."

"Maybe we'll be planning another one soon, then," Jackie teased and laughed as Helena blushed and waved a dismissing hand at her.

A couple of hours later, after Marc had been put to bed, the three of them sat in the living room, making plans, when the doorbell rang, interrupting their joyous preparations.

"I wonder who that could be," Helena murmured abstractedly as she got up to answer it. "I'm not expecting anyone."

A few minutes later she reappeared, a tall dark-haired attractive woman in tow, whose dark eyes fastened immediately onto Adam, their expression painfully revealing. Jackie knew without being told that this was the Miss Bowie whom he had been thinking about marrying, and she was seized with a combination of nervous jealousy and unwilling compassion for the woman whose hopes were about to be disappointed.

Adam got to his feet, his expression calm and gently welcoming. "Hello, Ruth," he said quietly, and then as Ruth's eyes swung to Jackie, he introduced the two of them with a minimum of fuss. "Ruth, this is Jackie Roth. Jackie...Ruth Bowie."

Jackie nodded as she got to her feet, her smile hesitant. "Hello, Ruth," she said quietly, then looked at Adam, begging him with her eyes to make this announcement as quickly as possible—and in private, to spare Ruth any humiliation

Helena stepped in to aid the process. "Jackie, why don't you come out to the kitchen with me to make coffee," she suggested warmly.

"Yes," Jackie answered gratefully, noting that Ruth must already suspect what was coming, since her face was pale and her hands were trembling slightly. The woman had eyes for no one but Adam, and as Jackie looked at the man she loved she realized how painful the next few moments were going to be for him. Then she turned her back and followed Helena out into the kitchen, suddenly seized with doubts that she deserved her own happiness when it would come at someone else's expense.

Once in the kitchen she gazed at Helena, her feelings apparent in her expressive eyes. "Don't worry, Jackie," Helena whispered softly. "If Adam had really loved Ruth, he would have married her long before now. He's had ample opportunity to do so. And anyone who sees the way he looks at you can't help but know that he does love you...not her."

"I suppose so," Jackie said weakly. "But I feel so guilty! I've already had so much love, and now I'm taking hers away from her!"

"No," Helena said firmly. "It wasn't there to take away. If Adam had married Ruth, it would only have been because he wanted marriage and children and because he likes her. That just isn't good enough. Believe me, I know!"

Jackie searched Helena's firm gaze for reassurance and found it, then the two of them swung to face the door when it burst inward and Ruth entered the room, tears in her eyes and anger in every line of her body.

"You!" She pointed at Jackie with a shaking finger. "You've stolen him from me!" And then she collapsed into tears as Adam came up behind her, his face revealing his distress and his compassion.

"She didn't, Ruth," he said gently, taking Ruth's shaking shoulders into his strong hands. "I fell in love with her . . . and she loves me. It's as simple as that."

"Simple!" Ruth twisted out of his hold and laughed half-hysterically. "If I'd known that canceling your reservation at that cursed mountain cabin wouldn't work, I'd have gone with you instead of waiting here like a fool while the two of you were—were—" She dissolved into tears again while Jackie watched, her soft heart torn by the hurt she had inadvertently inflicted on the other woman. But Adam, at seeing the sympathy in her eyes, gave Jackie a stern look that said more clearly than words that she had nothing to reproach herself for.

Nevertheless, his tone was gentle as he took hold of Ruth's shoulders again. "Come on, Ruth," he said quietly. "Let me take you home. You're too upset to drive."

"Upset?" Ruth laughed half-hysterically again, her eyes flashing fire as she pulled out of his hold. "You were ready to marry *me*, Adam!" she gasped out. *"Me*—not *her!"* She flung out a contemptuous hand at Jackie. Then she turned tortured eyes back to Adam. "I could have made you love me once we were married, Adam. I know I could have," she said in almost a begging tone. Her words died away, however, as she saw the inflexible look in Adam's eyes.

"I love Jackie, Ruth" was all he said, but he said it with such conviction in his quiet tone that all hope drained out of the woman's eyes.

With a gasping sob she turned and ran to the back door to fling herself out of the house, her sobbing echoing behind her like an accusation in Jackie's ears. But when Jackie turned to beg Adam to go after Ruth, her look faintly accusing that he couldn't have been more compassionate than to bludgeon the woman with the fact that he didn't love her, Adam stepped to her side, his gaze implacable as he held her own.

"She'll get over it faster knowing there's no hope," he said gently. "She'll be all right." He took Jackie's shoulders in his hands and looked down at her, his gaze level. "And I don't want you letting the fact that she's hurt now give you any second thoughts. You're mine. You're going to stay mine."

As Jackie looked up at him, despite her guilt feelings about Ruth, she knew he was right. She and Adam loved each other and they belonged together, and no one should be allowed to keep them apart. She nodded her acceptance as Adam took her into his arms and held her tightly to him while Helena slipped out of the room. His kiss stilled the last of Jackie's doubts, and she melted when he raised his head and, looking straight into her eyes, said, "I want you! I want you now!" his voice rasping with need.

"I want you, too, Adam," Jackie moaned fervently, needing him in all ways as she had never needed him before. She locked her arms around his neck and lifted herself on tiptoe to crush her mouth against his, showing him without further words exactly how much she wanted him.

A slight cough at the door broke up the embrace that was threatening to lead the two of them straight to the bedroom, and as Adam and Jackie turned their heads to where Helena stood in the door, eyeing them with mischievous gravity, their eyes had a mutually glazed, passionate expression that made Helena hesitate, then shrug her shoulders fatalistically.

"I was going to suggest we get on with the wedding plans, but—" Her raised eyebrows and rueful, quirking smile made Adam and Jackie each smile somewhat sheepishly.

Adam cleared his throat, but his voice was still somewhat hoarse as he replied. "We'll be right there, Helena," he said almost calmly. "Just give us a minute."

Helena grinned impishly as she raised her wrist and held it up to her eyes. She began counting the seconds off as she turned and left the room, and Adam's exasperated expression made Jackie laugh. "She's right, Adam," Jackie said regretfully. "We've very little time to make plans, and the sooner they're made, the sooner we can be together for good."

"That's a selfish attitude." He grinned, pleased apparently by that selfishness.

"Don't malign me," Jackie said with a pout, moving her hips deliciously against his. "I thought I'd already shown you how generous I can be."

"You have, darling," Adam agreed, his voice seductively low as his hands circled her bottom and lifted her up into the heat of his groin. "But I've got even more to give than you do," he added suggestively.

Feeling the burning, prodding heat of him, Jackie lifted lazy sensuous eyes to his and tried to make them widen in innocent amazement, though had she known it, her attempt at teasing was undermined by the wanting knowledge her look contained.

"Why, so you do," she breathed unsteadily, glorying in the frustrated longing she saw in his face. "How unfortunate that your gift will have to wait awhile."

"*Unfortunate* isn't the word for it." Adam growled his frustration as he leaned down to take a last kiss. "I never dreamed that when I finally fell hard for a woman, I'd get knocked right down to the ground. I'm so besotted with you, I'm even mad at Helena, and I haven't felt like that since she tried to ride my brand-new bicycle and scratched it up."

Jackie chuckled softly as she gave him one last longing, fervent hug. "In case you hadn't noticed, I'm not a bicycle," she teased. "I'm a lot softer, and my scratches heal . . . with a little help from a lover."

"Change that to a little help from *me*," Adam husked possessively. "I'm the only lover you're ever going to have from now on."

"You're the only lover I want," Jackie affirmed sincerely.

"Good," Adam answered with soft satisfaction. Then he sighed and moved away slightly. "All right." He groaned with fatalistic stoicism. "Let's get in there and get the preliminaries over with. I'm beginning to wish we'd stayed at the cabin. At least there I didn't have any competition when I wanted to make love to you."

Jackie laughed as she took his arm in her hands while they walked toward the door. "You don't have any competition now," she assured him dryly. "You just have interference."

"And that will stop three days from now," he assured her with a determination she couldn't dispute.

Though the next two days were hectic, as Jackie had to shop for a wedding dress, help Helena make arrangements for the wedding and Adam find the bare minimum of furnishings for their new home, Jackie found the time she needed to finish her wedding present for Adam. She revised her revisions, poured her heart into the relationship between the characters who represented herself and Adam, and hoped with every fiber of her being that Adam would overcome the negative reaction she expected in the first part of the book, where Matt resided.

The night before they were to be married she chose a moment when they were temporarily alone to present her gift—hesitantly, fearfully.

Adam took the box into his hands and eyed her uncustomary manner with fond discernment. "It's a book, isn't it?" he questioned gently.

Jackie nodded, licked her lips, and gathered her courage. "I—I'm not sure you'll like the first part,

Adam," she said as she looked up at him pleadingly. "But promise me you won't jump to any conclusions, or get too angry, and that you'll finish it?"

Adam reached a hand to tip her chin further and planted a warm kiss on her parted lips. "Darling Jack," he murmured huskily, his breathing made unsteady by the contact, since they hadn't been able to sleep together since arriving at his sister's. "You couldn't have chosen a gift I'd like better. I read somewhere that a writer's work is like a child to him, and until we have one of our own—until you can give me a living gift—I'm very happy that you've chosen to share this part of you with me."

Jackie smiled a little waveringly, hoping against hope that Adam's gratitude would survive the first chapter of the book, but confident that a man of his sensitivity and discernment couldn't fail to be pleased by the rest of the work in which he starred prominently.

"And now I have a gift for you," Adam continued, releasing her to reach into the pocket of his jacket. He withdrew a jeweler's box, the shape of which belied the fact that it held a ring.

"Oh, Adam," Jackie breathed pleasurably. "I'd forgotten all about a ring."

"Impertinent woman!" Adam teased gently. "How do you know it's not a pair of earrings?"

Jackie was already fumbling to open the small box, her fingers made clumsy by emotion. "You wouldn't dare!" she said in a choked voice, and then finally managed to open the box to discover a perfectly matched set of rings. "Ohhh..." she breathed ecstatically, pleased to the depths of her soul that Adam had chosen to wear a wedding ring himself.

The circles were intricately carved in an exquisite design, their soft gold shining in the light. "They're perfect, Adam...my darling, darling, Adam!" Jackie gasped, her eyes swimming over with tears as she leaned against the strength of the man she loved so desperately, she was afraid she might die of it. "I'm so glad you got one for you, too."

"I wanted to be sure that if any other judicial groupies show up in my courtroom, they'd know I was unavailable," Adam husked against her ear, cuddling her as best he could with one arm, the other still clutching his own gift. "The one I've got is all I can, or want, to handle."

The kiss they exchanged then was a promise, an exchange of breath and heart and soul—a shattering, warming, fulfilling expression of total love and commitment. When Adam at last drew back, his hazel eyes echoed the soft, passionate contentment in Jackie's blue ones.

"Thank God this is the last night we have to be apart," he said in a shaking voice. "And thank God you've given me some way to occupy myself through the long hours without you."

"You'd better get started, then," Jackie said, equally shaken. "I've got to go do some things to get ready for tomorrow myself."

And as Adam was moving away toward his room, his smile bathing her in a light that was especially his own, Jackie whispered soulfully, "I love you, Adam. I always will."

"I love you, too, Jack. And I always will." And then he was gone, leaving Jackie contented, frustrated, happy, anxious, aroused...unsated. She embraced each emotion in turn, thinking Adam Clarke was the only man in the world capable of bringing in his wake such conflict...and such happiness.

Chapter Thirteen

Swathed in luminescent pink that was so pale as to be almost white, Jackie peeked up from under her wide-brimmed hat at Adam's forceful, faintly stern profile, wishing she could be gifted in ESP and thereby know what he was thinking behind his dignified mask.

They were at the altar, listening to the minister begin the ceremony that would link them for the rest of their lives, or at least for as long as either of them lived, as Jackie had learned to think after having lost Matt long before her own life was over. And yet, at this moment, she wasn't sure that Adam viewed that prospect as favorably as he had the previous night, before she had given him her manuscript.

She hadn't so much as seen him, much less talked to him, since the preceding evening, and she longed to know his reaction to the book hadn't changed anything between them, that he understood what she had been trying to say and was pleased by what she *had* said.

They hadn't touched yet, unless she wanted to count the slight brushing of his impeccable suit sleeve against her bare arm, and she didn't. Cloth was no subtitute for the warm pulsing flesh that rested under it, and until Adam favored her with a direct look and the reassurance of his touch, she wouldn't be able to take as much joy in their mutual vows as she wanted with everything in her.

Jackie didn't have long to wait for the direct look. When the minister voiced the words that required her vow to love and to cherish Adam forever, she gazed up into the sparkling intensity of Adam's eyes and gave her answer with total commitment, using every nuance of tone and every bit of truth in her soul to convey to him that she meant her whispered yes every bit as fervently as the one she had given Matt.

Adam's expression reassured her, and when it came time to give his own answer, she would have had to have been deaf to miss the commitment in his own yes. It was only much later that it struck her that they had each, seemingly without volition and certainly without premeditation, chosen the one word for their answers, rather than the traditional "I do."

But yes was what they both meant—in all its connotations. They were each saying more than the one small word might convey to an outsider. They were saying yes to each other on every level that mattered, not simply making a legal commitment.

The rest of the ceremony passed in a blur for Jackie. She had eyes and ears only for Adam, secure now in her belief that he was still totally hers with no holding back. And all through the reception that followed she moved as though in a dream, performing the necessary social amenities punctiliously, even charmingly, while keeping an eye out for her husband, an ear for his voice, her heart and awareness resting in his keeping.

It was not until much later, when they were finally alone, ensconced in his new home, which was adequately, though sparsely furnished, and which had charmed her from the first moment she'd seen it, that Jackie was able to hear and touch and feel the man without any diversions to interfere.

"Adam," she protested without fervor when he picked her up to carry her over the threshold. "Don't you dare hurt your back. Not tonight!"

"I doubt your one hundred or so pounds are going to strain me," he responded tenderly. "And I'm not giving up this particular prerogative. I've been looking forward to it for thirty-seven years, and it's not my fault you waited until I was out of my prime to show up and put me out of my misery."

"If this is not prime," Jackie murmured meaningfully, running her hands over his broad shoulders, "then I'll take whatever cut it is. It can't be improved upon."

Adam set her down, folded her into his arms, and gave her her first kiss in her new home, a kiss that told her of his unleashed hunger and that sparked an answering response in her that threatened to have them consummating their marriage before they had taken two steps inside their new abode.

"Adam..." Jackie groaned against his mouth, trying to pull back, but finding he stymied her half-hearted effort with sinful ease. "We have champagne,

I have a beautiful new nightgown, and the floor is so hard.''

"Jack," he murmured, making no attempt to release her, "I'm hungry. Are you going to start off our marriage by refusing to feed me?"

"No, darling," Jackie promised, wrapping her arms around his neck and covering his face with kisses. "I'm just trying to whet your appetite."

"It doesn't need it. I'm ravenous!" he protested, pulling her even closer to him.

"Trust me," she whispered, staring soulfully into his eyes. "There's always room for growth in the human soul."

"I'm not talking about my soul," he rasped, but he did release his hold, however fractionally.

"I'm not either, not really." She smiled shimmeringly at him.

"I didn't think you could have changed that much in a few days," he said with satisfaction. "You have a lusty appetite of your own, if I recall, and I do, but I want to refresh my memory—now!"

"Okay, I'll race you to the bedroom," Jackie teased.

"I'd win," Adam demurred, "and I don't want to. This is one race I want to end in a tie."

"But you'll be operating under a handicap," Jackie said innocently.

"What handicap?" Adam was skeptical.

"You have to divert to the kitchen to get the champagne and glasses," she told him triumphantly, taking advantage of his momentary laxness to break his hold and back away.

Adam groaned, then sighed, then capitulated. "All

right, Mrs. Clarke. If you're that set on all the trappings, I'd be a heel to deny you them. But they'd better be short," he warned threateningly.

"And sweet," Jackie promised over her shoulder as she hurried toward the bedroom. She wanted an opportunity to wear the dream of a nightgown she'd found by sheer luck on her first visit to the lingerie department of a local store, even if she was under no illusions as to how long she would wear it.

Upon entering the one room she and Adam had managed to furnish completely, Jackie eyed the decor appreciatively, feeling satisfaction in the knowledge that she and the man she loved had similar tastes. The king-size bed, covered in a boldly striped spread, waited in patient splendor against one wall beside French doors leading to a private patio where she anticipated spending long summer evenings when the Montana winter was finally over. At one end of the room was a delightfully old-fashioned fireplace with a sofa in front of it and a comfortable lounging chair to one side. The chair had been chosen more for the fact that it would comfortably accommodate the two of them than for any other reason, but it fitted in with the rest of the furnishings quite nicely, its solid orange color picking up one of the stripes in the bedspread.

There was a huge handmade wardrobe Adam's father had made years before against one wall to contain Adam's clothing, while Jackie had the walk-in closet all to herself and a dresser in a wood to match the wardrobe.

The room was at once warmly solid, providing intimate sanctuary for the two of them, while the French doors and some plants Jackie had bought gave it a lighter air to relieve the overpowering size of the bed and the wardrobe. Adam was too big and very much too masculine to have felt comfortable in a more feminine room, while Jackie needed the lighter touches to keep from feeling overwhelmed. Their compromise had resulted in a room where both knew they would be able to spend hours of contentment and intimacy.

Jackie snatched her gown from her suitcase and was just disappearing into the bathroom when she heard the door opening to admit Adam into the bedroom. She eased the bathroom door shut and locked it, a gleeful smile parting her tender mouth.

"Where are you?" Adam shouted threateningly, his tone indicating disappointment that she had escaped him again.

"In the bathroom," Jackie carolled back. "I won!" She chuckled cheerfully as she pulled off her dress as fast as she was able.

"You cheated!" Adam growled in return, his voice coming closer to the bathroom door. A second later Jackie saw the handle of the door begin to turn in a stealthy manner.

"Sorry," she chortled. "I need privacy to get ready for my grand entrance. It's a good thing there's a sturdy lock on this door. I would have thought a judge would understand a person's right to privacy once in a while."

"Don't count on it." Adam was back to threats. "I'm handy enough with tools to get rid of every lock in the house."

"Not tonight," Jackie sang out on a warbling note.

"Jackie!" Adam's patience was definitely running out, and Jackie had to stifle a giggle.

"Got your jammies on, Adam?" she called, her mirth coloring her voice unmistakably.

"I don't wear *jammies*," Adam replied with withering disgust. "And if I did, it wouldn't be worth it to waste my time putting them on—not tonight!" And he added with sly purpose, "Just like it won't be worth your while putting on a nightgown."

"Nevertheless," Jackie said, opening the door with a flourish and posing for him with all the seductive slinkiness she could manage, "it *is* on. What do you think of it?"

Adam blinked, very slowly, and then a bemused smile curved his mouth. "I think you're enchanting," he said with such total sincerity that Jackie started melting all the way down to her toes.

The gown was blue, matching her eyes perfectly, and it fit everywhere it should, and even a few places where it shouldn't. It was such a combination of provocative sexuality and innocent purity that Adam could be forgiven if he couldn't take his eyes off it and what it concealed—or didn't conceal.

"May I have a glass of champagne, Adam?" Jackie inquired softly, her heart beginning a deep rhythm that made the gown move beguilingly over her breasts.

"Hmmm?" Adam responded absently, then tore his eyes from her form to lift them to hers. "Ummm-hmmm," he murmured, just as absently.

He started moving backward, slowly, never taking his eyes off Jackie. When he got to the bedside table, where the champagne rested, he fumbled with the bottle and glasses until Jackie was sure he wouldn't manage to pour without spilling, but somehow he did.

Holding her glass out toward her, he invited huskily, "Come and get it."

She glided to where he stood, stopped just out of reach, and took the glass, holding his eyes with her own while she sipped delicately. "Aren't you going to have any, darling?" she queried softly, a tender smile curving her mouth into a delicious temptation.

Adam's eyes were riveted to her mouth, and his strangled "What?" was barely audible.

"Champagne," she reminded him, her breathing making it difficult to frame the word.

"Oh," he said, looking down at his glass as though he couldn't remember that he held anything. Then a smile appeared, and he glanced up at her with eyes glitteringly purposeful. "Yes, I think I will."

Instead of drinking he dipped a finger into the glass, then carried the droplets of champagne to Jackie's trembling mouth, moving closer as he did so, gently coating her lips with the cool liquid. Then his mouth descended until he was close enough to very delicately, very erotically lick the drops from her parted lips with a tongue grown diabolical in its purpose.

"Oh, God, Adam!" Jackie murmured, leaning into him, all inclination toward teasing fled into oblivion. "Please..."

He didn't need a second invitation. The glasses were set aside, Jackie was scooped up into his arms and deposited onto the bed, and Adam was out of his clothes and beside her in the time it took her to take three deep breaths to calm her rapidly deteriorating control.

"Now, Mrs. Clarke," Adam rasped as he covered her body with his own. "You've had my gentle, tender seductions. This time you're going to find out what I'm like when I'm near starvation and have been thwarted for much too long by my wife's misguided sense of humor."

"Yes, Adam..." Jackie pleaded on a rising note of desperate love and desire. Then she was rendered speechless by a plundering mouth and a passion-driven body that delivered what it promised with interest.

Jackie found the strength and the temporary clarity of thought to ask a question that had been bothering her so strongly at their wedding.

"Adam," she ventured hesitantly, her voice muffled against his chest.

"Ummm?" he answered with satisfied laziness, stroking her body with possessive hands.

"Did you like the book, Adam?" she queried tentatively.

Adam stayed silent for so long that Jackie began to despair of a positive answer. But then he lifted her chin so that she had to raise her head to face his eyes head on. What she saw there both reassured and confused her. There was love and possessiveness and regret and force in his look.

"I think Matt Roth was one of the luckiest, and the unluckiest, men to have ever walked this earth," he told her sincerely. "I'm jealous of what you had together in a way, but I can't justify my jealousy, so I've decided not to give in to it. I'm sorry he died, but I'm not sorry I'm alive to benefit from his absence. And if he were alive right now, I wouldn't give you up to him. You're mine now, and it's possible that I love you so much partially because of the years you spent with him. If so, I'm grateful. But it really doesn't matter one way or the other. I do love you, I do intend to keep you, and—" He paused, and gradually his seriousness changed to his customary humor. "And if I'm anywhere near as wonderful as you painted me in the book, I shouldn't have any trouble doing just that."

As Jackie breathed a deep sigh of relief, gazing at him with all her love in her eyes, he took her chin in his hand, and his eyes grew serious again. "You have a tremendous talent for writing, Jackie. You know I won't object if you intend to keep on with it, don't you?"

Jackie nodded, her heart swelling with grateful love at his understanding that she would always want to practice her profession. "Now that I've actually written a whole book instead of just an article, I want to try it again. This time I'll write the book I had intended to write before you came on the scene," she said tenderly.

"Good," he murmured, his eyes beginning to take on the special glow of hunger again—hunger for her. "Now can we concentrate on the present?" he demanded gently, moving closer to enfold her in his arms. "Someday we can talk about Matt as easily and naturally as he deserves. And we can talk about your writing every day if you like. But right now..." His lips began to caress and tantalize hers, and Jackie's mouth responded by molding itself to his with exquisite compatibility.

For long moments the room was filled with a silence that was only broken by sighs, gasps, and their mingled breathing, which was growing more audible by the moment. Then Adam drew his head back slightly from ravaging Jackie's willing mouth and he muttered huskily, "I didn't mean you couldn't talk at all," he said meaningfully. "I need to hear you tell me you love me. I want to hear how much you want me—in detail—and I want to hear you say you're all mine now."

"I am, Adam," Jackie assured him with husky aroused tenderness. "I'm all yours...."

And then she set about proving it with delicate, passionate love in every gesture, every movement, every word she whispered to him to encourage him to take what was his alone, finally driving him over the edge of restraint until he reciprocated in his own masterful fashion. Together they laid to rest every doubt that had ever been between them, and went on to capture a new height to their relationship that was all the more satisfying when both knew they could reach it again and again.

When at last Jackie snuggled against her new husband's side, drained and exhausted and utterly contented, she had time for one last thought before she drifted into sleep on this, her second wedding night. She reminded herself that she must remember to call

Dr. Chelski and tell him that the hunting in Wyoming had been exceptionally good this year, and that she had, indeed, found a younger, sexier man to whisper sweet nothings into her ear from now until there was no longer any breath for Adam to speak them, nor her own eager ear to hear them.

Harlequin reaches
into the hearts and minds
of women across America
to bring you

Harlequin American Romance™·

YOURS FREE!

Enter a uniquely exciting new world with

Harlequin American Romance T.M.

Harlequin American Romances are the first romances to explore today's love relationships. These compelling novels reach into the hearts and minds of women across America... probing the most intimate moments of romance, love and desire.

You'll follow romantic heroines and irresistible men as they boldly face confusing choices. Career first, love later? Love without marriage? Long-distance relationships? All the experiences that make love real are captured in the tender, loving pages of **Harlequin American Romances**.

What makes American women so different when it comes to love? Find out with **Harlequin American Romance!**

Send for your introductory **FREE** book now!

Get this book FREE!

Mail to:

Harlequin Reader Service

In the U.S.
2504 West Southern Avenue
Tempe, AZ 85282

In Canada
649 Ontario Street
Stratford, Ontario N5A 6W2

YES! I want to be one of the first to discover **Harlequin American Romance.** Send me FREE and without obligation *Twice in a Lifetime*. If you do not hear from me after I have examined my FREE book, please send me the 4 new **Harlequin American Romances** each month as soon as they come off the presses. I understand that I will be billed only $2.25 for each book (total $9.00). There are no shipping or handling charges. There is no minimum number of books that I have to purchase. In fact, I may cancel this arrangement at any time. *Twice in a Lifetime* is mine to keep as a FREE gift, even if I do not buy any additional books.

Name _____
                              (please print)

Address _____
                                              Apt. no.

City _____ State/Prov. _____ Zip/Postal Code _____

Signature (If under 18, parent or guardian must sign.)